WATCH
OUT
FOR JAMIE
JOEL

MIKE DUMBLETON

ALLEN&UNWIN

The writing of this book was assisted by the Government of South Australia through Arts South Australia

ARTSA Government of South Australia

First published in 2003
Copyright © Mike Dumbleton 2003

Allen & Unwin Pty Ltd
83 Alexander Street
Crows Nest NSW 2065
Australia
Phone: (61 2) 8425 0100
Fax: (61 2) 9906 2218
Email: frontdesk@allen-unwin.com.au
Web: http://www.allenandunwin.com

National Library of Australia
Cataloguing-in-publication entry:

Dumbleton, Mike.
  Watch out for Jamie Joel.

For young adults.
ISBN 1 86508 532 4.

1. Teacher–student relationships – Fiction. I. Title.

A823.3

Designed by Deborah Ladd, Traffic Design Studios
Typeset by Midland Typesetters
Printed by McPherson's Printing Group

10 9 8 7 6 5 4 3 2 1

MIKE DUMBLETON is a very tall, gentle, curly-haired person with a passion for basketball. He was born in England and came to Australia with his wife Linda in 1972. He was always interested in books and finally started writing his own when his children were nearly grown up and it was clear he wasn't getting any better at basketball. Since then he has published many educational resource books and picture books, including five Children's Book Council Notable Books, and the 2002 shortlisted title, *Passing On*. *Watch Out for Jamie Joel* is his first novel for young adults.

Mike works as an English and Literacy Co-ordinator at an Adelaide high school. His long experience in schools and the many funny, touching or disturbing incidents he's witnessed are woven into this novel.

Apart from basketball, Mike's interests include jogging, swimming and watching soccer. He has his own website, at
www.mikedumbleton.cjb.net

*For the many teachers and students
who have been such a significant part of my life*

JAMIE

Key turning in the front door.

'Thank Christ for that, she's gone out,' came Pat's voice. 'It was like having your head tied to a loudspeaker when I left here.'

Footsteps went down the passage towards the kitchen.

'Make yourself comfy in the lounge, Deb, while I get us a cup of tea. With any luck she'll stay out a bit longer and give us some peace and quiet.'

'I know what you mean—' Pat's friend Debbie was at the doorway. Her thin lips formed an O of surprise. 'She's *here*!'

'What?'

'Jamie's here.'

Sharp banging of drawers and clatter of mugs and spoons. Pat appeared with a tray.

'Sulking, are you? CD player broken, is it?' she sneered.

'I turned it *off*,' Jamie snapped.

'Nice of you to wait till I'm out of the house.'

'At least it's got an Off button, which is more than I can say for *you*.'

The tray tilted and tea slopped from one of the mugs. Pat's face seethed with anger.

'Sneaky little cow. Sitting here listening to other people's conversations.'

Jamie's lips jabbered like a frenzied fish – spontaneous mimicking.

Slap.

Pain raked her cheek. She clutched her face, feeling the smear of blood.

'Bitch!' Rage took over. *Punch*, *scratch*. 'Keep your friggin' hands off me.' Jamie's fingers hooked into Pat's blouse, ripping buttons out. She clawed forward, grasping at her hair.

Suddenly she was jerked back by Debbie, screeching, 'Stop it!'

Pat's face changed to triumph. She shoved her knuckles hard into Jamie's shoulder.

Jamie lurched free of both of them.

'It's *your* turn now, I s'pose?' She speared the question at Debbie. 'So Pat'll hold me while *you* have a swing.'

Debbie fidgeted awkwardly.

Jamie charged past Pat.

'Where d'you think you're going?'

'As if you care.'

Slam. The front door rattled behind her.

Time to get out of there. Away, anywhere.

 CRAIG ELIOT

Week 1 as deputy principal, and I think I could be living in the shadow of my predecessor.

I asked Greg Proden if he enjoyed teaching Social Studies.

'Too late for a career change now,' he said. 'But it's okay if the deadheads are under control.'

'And how do you make sure of that?'

'I send them to you.' He put his coffee cup under the urn and pressed the hot water button. 'What's your attitude to troublemakers?' he asked pointedly.

'They need sorting out,' I replied ambiguously. I knew the answer would be relayed to other staff as soon as I'd gone, and I didn't want to be labelled before I'd even started the job.

Greg nodded, but I could see he wasn't convinced. I'd be on trial from day one as far as he was concerned. 'Gerald Strehborn had the right idea. Stamp on the smart-arses and kick them out if they cause problems.'

'How long have you been teaching here?' I asked.

'Too long.'

I was tempted to agree with him.

Gary Hawthorne, one of the Tech. Studies teachers, came to see me about having too many kids on his Year 10 class list. He said it was a safety issue. He was pretty uptight. Apparently the kids welded his bag closed in metalwork last year, then they nicked half his equipment, dropping it out the window and collecting it at recess.

Mrs Horrowitz came to see me because she didn't want me to get the wrong idea about her son Danny. She said people picked on Danny just because he was prepared to stand up for himself. She and her boyfriend had made things very clear to Danny. He wasn't to cause any trouble, but he wasn't to 'take any shit'.

Warren, his younger brother, is starting here this year. He's been given the same advice.

I talked to some of the staff about Mrs Horrowitz. Apparently, 'taking no shit' means not working, not listening, and threatening violence whenever you can't get your own way.

Angela Davis, the school counsellor, was flat out with enrolments this morning, so I offered to help by seeing Mrs Lee and her son Aaron.

Mrs Lee looked worn and nervous. She fiddled with her lighter, turning it over and tapping it on her knee.

'His father doesn't know where we are,' she said. 'If anyone phones, asking about Aaron, people mustn't say he's here. We had a lot of trouble at the last school.'

Aaron sat with his arms folded.

'His father's violent. We've got a restraining order against him, but it didn't make any difference at my sister's, so we're staying with someone he doesn't know.'

Mrs Lee tapped her knee again. 'The last time he found us, he paid some kids to hassle us at night. They smashed windows and rocked the roof, swearing and carrying on. Aaron was terrified. My sister was crying. We shouldn't have to put up with that.'

'Does your husband have any idea where you are now?'

'I don't think so. I didn't tell anyone. Not even my sister.' She patted Aaron's knee. 'We'll be okay, won't we, Aaron?'

'Well, it sounds as though things are going to settle down,' I responded encouragingly. 'And Aaron can get on with his schooling.'

I smiled at Aaron, but he went on staring at the floor.

'He's a bit nervous,' Mrs Lee offered. 'He does his best, but he's been away a lot.'

'Now's a great time to be starting,' I emphasised. 'All the Year 8s are new, so Aaron'll be the same as everybody else.'

I showed Aaron where to report on the first day and said I'd be around if he had any questions.

As they headed out to the street, I saw Mrs Lee put her arm around Aaron's shoulder and ruffle his red hair.

I made a note to tell staff not to release any information

about Aaron over the phone, and to ask Angela to set up a meeting with Mrs Lee. She needed all the support we could give her.

There's already something on my desk about Danny and Warren Horrowitz, and the students aren't even back at school yet. The PE shed was broken into during the holidays and the groundsman left a note to say that they were hanging around the school and they'd either done it or 'damn well' knew who had.

I can see it's going to be difficult to get a balanced view of the school in this job. The only kids I've heard about so far are the ones who cause trouble. Thank goodness I've got an English class. It'll remind me that some kids can behave normally.

The CD cases clattered as Jamie flipped them forward. She loved the pulsing rhythms of the dance mix pounding from the speakers in the store – music you could bury yourself in.

'That's crap.'

Ricky's shaved head appeared over the top of the stand in front of her, grinning.

'That's crap, that is.'

Jamie smiled. 'I was thinking of buying it for you.'

'Don't!' Ricky shook his head. 'If you want it for your birthday, I can get it for free.'

She pushed his shoulder. 'You can't nick 'em, because they're kept behind the counter.'

Ricky rolled his eyes. 'I can't believe this. Would I nick CDs? Me?'

He paused, then leaned forward and said in a stage whisper. 'I just nick the money, then I buy them like everyone else.'

Jamie laughed. She'd known Ricky for ever. He was always like this. Smart answers and jokes, never anything serious.

'Where are the others?'

Ricky pointed towards the Mall. 'There's only Paula and Dominic around.'

Jamie was about to ask, *Dominic who?* when Paula appeared.

They hugged, then Paula turned to introduce Dominic.

'Dominic, Jamie,' Paula indicated, flicking her hair away from her face.

'Hello,' Dominic smiled.

He was older than she was, and taller. He remained still, just looking at her. He had straw-coloured dreadlocks and pale skin – and a small dragon pendant around his neck.

'He's a friend of Ricky's,' Paula whispered as the boys drifted towards the counter.

Jamie gave her a searching look.

'No, nothing like that.' Paula shook her head. 'I'm trying to get on with Kane. You know that. I don't just jump at anyone who comes along. What do you think I am?'

'Pass,' said Jamie.

Paula grinned. 'What happened to you?' She pointed to the cut on Jamie's cheek.

'Pat. And Debbie.'

'Bitch! Poor you.'

The main entrance to the Mall opened and closed continuously, like huge jaws. Late-night shoppers streamed in and out. Jamie recognised a boy in her year level, struggling with an ever-lengthening chain of shopping trolleys. He saw them watching and looked away.

Over the afternoon, Jamie had found out more about Dominic. He was Ricky's cousin. He'd left home, left school and now worked late shifts at some chicken place.

They were crowded along a table at the side of the food court, where they could see everyone who went by.

'Had some trouble with my stepdad.' Dominic glanced at the cut on Jamie's face. 'Too many rules. Too hands-on.'

'Speaking of rules – I collected my schoolbooks this morning. Saw the new deputy,' interrupted Ricky. 'He was reading a pile of your old detention slips.'

Ricky had no sense of timing. Ignore him.

'Will you go back home?' she asked Dominic.

Dominic shook his head. 'I won't stay long at Ricky's either. Just till I sort something out.' He glanced at his watch. 'Have to go. My shift starts at eight.' He eased himself off the bench they were sitting on. 'You look cold.'

Hard to deny it with her arms crossed, clasping collarbones.

Dominic slipped his jacket round her shoulders. Not quite a matador, but close.

'No! I'm okay, really. Anyway, you can't leave it here.'

'Give it to Ricky later on. It's no big deal.' He gave a sort of half-wave which included everybody. 'See you later.'

'See ya later, man.'

'Bye.'

'Thanks.'

The group was breaking up, but there was no way Jamie was going home until Pat was asleep. She'd go to Paula's place and stay as long as possible. If Paula's parents didn't give her a lift, she'd make the best of walking home in the dark. Pat usually took a tablet at about ten o'clock and was asleep before ten-thirty. In some ways she was more like an old granny than an aunt.

Jamie eased her arms into the cavernous sleeves of Dominic's jacket. She pulled the cuffs back, plunged her hands into the pockets and wrapped her arms across her body.

She felt a flush of warmth, deep inside.

'Kids asleep?'

'Marc might still be awake. I've only just put him down.' Nicole remained seated, watching the TV.

'Are you okay?'

'I'm exhausted. Renae didn't sleep all day, so I didn't get any breaks at all.'

I dropped my bag and crept into the children's bedroom. Light from the hallway spread across Marc's bed. He was fast asleep. His sit-on car was next to the bed, and his cuddly dog, Clem, was tucked in with him, one floppy ear across Marc's face. I caught the smell of shampoo as I kissed Renae's baby forehead.

This is the fourth night in a row I've been home late. Last night, Nicole was asleep as well, flaked out on the lounge.

This job is unrelenting. I can see how much I'd taken for granted in my old school. Student information, staff information, policy decisions, timetables, curriculum options, room allocations, discipline procedures, fire drills, assembly arrangements, special events, meeting schedules, committees, sub-committees, task groups; there's no end to it. The principal is supportive and it's good to have the extra money, but already there are times when I wonder if it's worth it.

Things were frantic again today. We had a heap of new enrolments – kids who moved into the area during the holidays and just turned up on the first day of school. Several had shifted from one parent to the other in split families, and at least half had been to three or more schools in the last few years. I'm sure some of them will have gone again before the term's finished.

Aaron Lee's still here, and so is his mum. When I saw her in the yard this morning, I thought she'd come for an appointment with the counsellor.

'Hello! Are you looking for Ms Davis's office?'

'No, not today,' she smiled. 'I've just volunteered to help out in the canteen. I'm starting tomorrow.' Her voice was chirpy and bright. 'It's great. I'll get to know people. And I can keep an eye on Aaron.'

'How's Aaron going?' I asked. 'Has he settled in okay?'

'Really well. He's even made a friend – Warren something.'

'Warren Horrowitz?'

'That's it. Warren Horrowitz. What's he like?'

'I haven't actually met him yet,' I replied, ignoring the alarm bells going off inside my head. 'It takes a while to get to know all the new students.'

The canteen ladies are a cheerful bunch. They've all got kids at the school except for Sharleen, the manageress. Sharleen's daughter left some time ago.

I went over with a late lunch order, after recess. I explained that Marc had been ill during the night and that Nicole needed help getting both the kids ready for an early doctor's appointment. In the rush to get away, I'd left my sandwiches in the fridge.

'We'll forgive you this time,' chided one of the ladies.

'So you're the new deputy,' said another. 'We've heard all about you.'

'Who from?'

'The kids at recess. There's not much we don't know about here,' laughed Sharleen. 'We get all the gossip.'

'I'll remember that,' I smiled, handing over my lunch order. 'Is the information free or do I have to pay for it?'

'It all depends,' grinned Sharleen, nudging the woman next to her, 'on whether or not you keep putting in late lunch orders.'

I was surprised when I saw Danny Horrowitz for the first time. With the amount of trouble he was supposed to cause around the school, I expected him to be big and tough. He isn't. He's skinny with fair hair. His shoulders are slightly rounded, and he looks quite mild.

'Do you know anything about the sports shed being broken into during the holidays, Danny?'

'The groundsman's a wanker. What's he said?'

'Danny, the groundsman is called Mr Harris and I didn't ask for your opinion about him. If I ever do, that's not the way I expect you to talk.'

'He just wants to get me into trouble. What'm I s'posed to say if he is a wanker?'

'I can see you don't want to discuss this now, Danny, and I've got things to do, so I'll find somewhere for you to wait, then we'll try again at recess.'

'It wasn't anyone from this school.'

'So you know who it was?'

'No.'

'If anyone knows what's going on round here, Danny, I imagine it's you. And if you don't know, I think you can find out.'

'I've been trying to find out.'

'Well, that's good, Danny. If you do find out who did it, you can let me know.'

'Oh yeah. Good one,' he said bluntly. 'Like I wanna get my head kicked in.'

'So why have you been trying to find out who did it, then, Danny?'

'Because I want a new basketball.'

I made a note to watch Danny carefully. Any sign of a new basketball, and he'd be taken in for questioning.

Jamie was late, hurrying. Good thing the Marlows lived just around the corner.

Babysitting the Marlow kids could be depressing. Alex, the older one, was out of control – a foul-mouthed, feral brat. Just as well Cheryl didn't expect her to keep track of him. Sometimes she heard Cheryl going off her head at Alex over the back fence.

Most kids waited until secondary school before they dropped out. Alex had dropped out years ago. She'd seen his mother drag him into primary school, but it never lasted. He was always racing off on his bike.

'Hello! It's only me.' Jamie pulled back the screen door. The front door was already open.

The crying started immediately.

'Is that you, Jamie? . . . Come in. I'm nearly ready. Heath, get off!'

The crying became desperate.

It was always the same. Jamie followed the noise to the bedroom. Cheryl was in front of the mirror, trying to put the finishing touches to her make-up.

Heath clung to her leg, eyes creased with tears. He tightened his grip and buried his face in her skirt when he saw Jamie.

'Heath! You'll ladder my pantyhose.'

Cheryl moved stiffly away from the mirror with Heath attached, like someone with a wooden leg. She picked up her jacket and handbag from the bedside chair.

Heath screamed.

Cheryl struggled to prise his fingers off the hem of her skirt. Her face was distraught. When she worked split shifts at the pub, she went through this routine twice a day.

Cheryl was trapped and she knew it.

It was a life Jamie never ever wanted to live.

Alex wheeled his bike to the bedroom, pushing doors open with the front tyre.

'Shh! You'll wake him up.' Jamie pointed to Heath, asleep on the floor.

'If he stays there, I'll tread on him,' Alex grunted.

He might mean it. He had a foul temper. There were some new holes in the lounge wall and another in the kitchen, low down by the fridge.

Jamie lifted Heath gently, and carried him to the mattress in Cheryl's room. Anything for a quiet life.

Alex reappeared and slumped into a chair.

'Where've you been?'

'None of your business, Nosy,' said Alex.

Jamie shrugged.

Alex pulled a CD player out of his pocket and unravelled the headphones.

'D'you want one of these? I can get it for ya cheap.'

Jamie shook her head. 'I'd rather have something the police aren't looking for.'

'If you know anyone who wants a cheap basketball, I can get them as well,' said Alex.

Jamie showed no interest.

'I'm at your school now,' Alex continued.

'Haven't seen you there.'

'I stick with me mates. Mum's pleased because I've been every day.'

Alex was talking crap. Jamie knew it. He hadn't even been to the first assembly.

'What d'you think of it?' she asked.

'It's all right.'

'What about that stupid yellow skirt the new deputy wears?'

'She's a full-on lesbian,' replied Alex without hesitation.

'And you're a total liar,' triumphed Jamie. 'The new deputy's a man!'

'Think you're smart,' Alex sneered.

He went quiet. Jamie could see him trying to think of something to say, to re-establish himself in the conversation.

'You got a boyfriend?'

Jamie thought of Dominic. She shook her head.

'Mum has. He's called Rob.'

'What's he like?'

'He likes havin' it off with Mum. That's what he likes,' Alex sniggered. 'I've heard 'em sometimes. It's disgustin'.'

Jamie didn't know what to say.

'Mum's not the only one,' continued Alex. 'I seen him with someone else, comin' out of the bar at the Footy Club.'

'That doesn't mean anything.'

'He had his arm round her and he was chewin' her neck,' said Alex emphatically.

'Have you told your mum?'

'Nah. I've got a better idea.'

'What's that?'

'I'm gonna tell Rob I know and make some money out of it.'

I met Jamie Joel today. I'd been warned about her. I saw a neat, slim, dark-haired girl, looking at a noticeboard near the Physics lab. She started to move away when she saw me.

'Excuse me. What's your name?'

'Natalie.'

'Natalie who?'

'Cromar,' she smiled.

She spoke with poise and confidence.

'Well, Natalie, it's lesson time now, so where are you supposed to be?'

'Senior school study. I left something in my locker. I'm going back now.'

'Okay.' I nodded sympathetically.

'Jamie! You're supposed to be over here.' Jessica Rowan pointed to a spot next to her doorway, then returned to the room.

Jamie sheepishly moved as directed, dark hair screening her face.

'I think we'd better start again . . . Jamie. Why are you here?'

'It was a mistake. Mrs Rowan got things wrong. We're going to sort it out at recess.'

'What kind of mistake? Was it like deliberately giving a false name?'

Jamie was quick to ask what it had to do with me. I reminded her that student behaviour management was my job, and that part of the issue was now her identity crisis in the corridor. From the way she looked at me, I had the distinct feeling that it wasn't possible to be a deputy and a human being at the same time.

Jessica Rowan spotted me outside the room. 'It's okay,

I can deal with it,' she said. 'Jamie can come back when she's made a full written apology—'

'I didn't say it to you.' Jamie crossed her arms angrily and turned away.

'As I was saying,' Mrs Rowan continued calmly, 'when she's made a full written apology, with a guarantee that it won't happen again.'

'I was just reading what was on the desk.'

'In that case, Jamie,' said Mrs Rowan quietly, 'if you see "You're an F'head" written on a desk in future, I suggest that you clean it off straight away rather than reading it out at the top of your voice when a teacher enters the room.'

It wasn't supposed to be like this. She'd planned to stay out of trouble. This was her new start, and for three days it had gone okay. Now she'd blown it.

Jamie looked up at the new deputy talking quietly to Mrs Rowan. He was nicer-looking than Strehborn, younger and with more hair. Strehborn was a stumpy little troll with stick-out, marble eyes. But it didn't make any difference. They were all the same.

He'd recognised her real name. He knew the surname without asking. Strehborn had probably left a photo, blown up to the size of a Wanted poster, with detailed notes on all her sins.

Jamie wondered what was in the notes. Were they full of all that teacher stuff that never quite said what happened? Did they use words like 'disruptive', 'unco-operative', 'inappropriate' – the kind of things that were usually scrawled on detention and yard duty slips? Or did Strehborn have a big spit before he left, and really get things off his chest?

Perhaps he wrote, 'Watch out for Jamie Joel. She's a right little smart-arse who always gets into trouble then argues black and blue it was nothing to do with her. She's got a real temper and a mouth like a sewer when she gets going.'

Jamie looked round at the sound of the classroom door closing. The deputy's footsteps echoed lightly along the corridor as he walked away. He was going straight back to the office to read Strehborn's notes again.

Jamie could feel her temper ease gradually, so that she was able to separate her thoughts from her reactions. It was like focusing a video camera on herself, watching what she was doing. Jamie cam'. Now she could see herself from the outside, hunched against the corridor wall, and it wasn't the picture she wanted. It reminded her of a beggar she'd seen in the city, curled up in a doorway trying to keep out the cold.

At least she had a picture. That was a start. It gave her the chance to think about what she was doing. To sort herself out. Then she could try to adjust the picture into something she did want to see.

Jamie straightened her back. That was better. Less pathetic.

Everything had been going well for the first couple of days. She'd done what she told herself to do in the holidays. She'd started all her classes without drawing attention to herself. Then this happened. Outside the room she could admit it was stupid. The picture she had of herself was on slow-motion replay. She was lucky it was Mrs Rowan. At least she'd talk to you first.

A door opened down the corridor and a younger kid came out.

'So why's it just me? What about him?' he shouted.

'Just get out.'

The door banged shut. The boy twisted his shoulders

around, kicked the wall and swore under his breath. She recognised him. Warren Horrowitz, Danny's brother. Little brat. She passed their place every day on the way to school.

Warren turned and slouched with his back against the wall. He kicked it several times with the heel of his shoe. Pause. Then a series of dull thuds, as he stabbed back against the wall with the fleshy side of his fists.

She watched him lean back and slide slowly onto the floor. His legs unfolded and stuck out into the corridor. The corridor went quiet again.

I left a note at the canteen, asking Mrs Lee to catch up with me when she had a spare moment. I made a point of saying there was nothing to worry about, I just needed to check some information, but she still looked apprehensive, perched on the edge of her chair.

'Is Aaron okay?'

'Yes. He's fine.'

'We had a phone call earlier that I wanted to ask you about.'

Mrs Lee looked at me warily.

'Who was it?'

'I don't know exactly. Someone phoned the front office, asking if we had a new kid at the school called Wayne Shaw.'

I paused. No reaction.

'It was a man's voice,' I continued. 'He said he was the boy's uncle.'

Mrs Lee held my gaze, rubbing the back of her hand. 'Why are you telling me?'

'Because he described the boy as being shy, skinny and pale, with red hair.'

She leaned forward, urgently.

'Did they say he was here? What did they say?'

'Nothing. It's all okay. He was told it was Department policy not to release information like that. We couldn't say whether a particular student was here or not.'

'Was he suspicious?'

'I don't think so. It sounds as though he'd had the same response from other schools. He was abusive instead.'

Mrs Lee shrugged and sat back.

'I still haven't told my sister where we are. He's just ringing all the schools, hoping to strike lucky. . . . Aaron doesn't have to know about this, does he?'

'I won't be saying anything,' I assured her.

'Thanks.' She managed a smile as she stood up to leave. 'It's just that things are beginning to work out. I like being Mrs Lee, and Way . . he likes being Aaron.'

Before I could get to any paperwork, the receptionist phoned to say the police had arrived with two of our students and wanted to speak to me.

The boys grinned foolishly at one another as they entered my office. From the way the receptionist spoke, I had a strong feeling they were regular visitors to the front office and that I'd be seeing them again before long.

One of the officers took out his notes as he sat down.

'We received a call from the manager of the recycling depot in Wilton at 10.15 this morning. He'd caught these two boys gaining money under false pretences. They've given their names as Jason Gillet and Shaun Neale.' He looked at me for confirmation.

I nodded, 'That's right.' I had their files in front of me.

The policeman pointed to Jason.

'Jason here can tell you what they've been up to.'

Jason squirmed and shuffled his feet. Shaun looked away.

'We took some bottles,' Jason mumbled. He looked sideways at the policeman.

'Go on.'

'They was empty bottles.'

'Go on.'

'We took them in to get the money back on them. And we got caught.'

I looked at the policeman, questioningly.

'That's right. They were caught nicking soft-drink bottles through a hole in the fence at the back of the depot and cashing them in round the front.'

Part of me wanted to laugh, but I kept a straight face as the policeman continued.

'The cashier got suspicious because Mr Coca-Cola and his mate here got too greedy. They started bringing hundreds of bottles round in shopping trolleys, every twenty minutes.'

It was getting harder to look stern, so I decided to move things on. I asked if the manager intended to press charges. The answer was no. The manager would press charges if it happened again. This time he wanted the school to know and the parents to be informed.

I assured the police that we would follow up on everything, including wagging school, which we hadn't even talked about yet.

It felt good having convinced the deputy that she was Natalie Cromar, even if it did only last for thirty seconds. Not everyone could get away with it. She *could* be a different person. It *was* possible.

'Anything's better than school.' That's what the real Natalie Cromar had said when she left last year.

She was wrong. Jamie had seen what *anything* looked like thirty years later. It looked like Pat.

Yesterday she'd even got through a lesson with Proden, despite the fact that he had a go at her straight away.

'You'll only be sitting there if you do the right thing. Any problems, and I'll move you.'

There were several things she wanted to say, none of them polite, but she managed to just shrug her shoulders and give him a look which said, 'Do what you like.'

She hated him. Prick. Some teachers went out of their way to say things like 'Hello, Jamie. How was the holiday?' They might not give a stuff, but at least it sounded friendly, as if they didn't mind her being there.

The new deputy seemed okay, really. Whatever he knew about her, he hadn't dragged it up straight away. No instant accusations.

Strehborn always used to raise his voice. He made loud comments about you to other teachers. He said things like, 'I think we have someone here who wants to leave school'. He was always doing things just to show everyone he was in charge.

Laughter – down the corridor. Warren was on his feet again, giving everybody the finger, through the window with both hands, several times.

More laughter.

Warren shot back, dropped to the floor and wrapped his arms around his knees. The teacher looked out.

'What have I done now?' protested Warren. 'S'pose I'm in trouble for doin' nothing again?'

'If you've been looking through the window, don't,' said the teacher. He pointed down the corridor to the opposite wall. 'Sit over there, then you won't get tempted.'

'Why? I haven't done anything.'

'Do as you're asked, please. Now!'

Warren grudgingly started to push with his feet so that he slid slowly across the floor on his backside, like a rower.

'Hurry up.'

'Yeah, yeah. Whatever you say.'

The teacher disappeared, shouting into the room, 'You've all got work to do. Why are you out of your places?'

The door closed.

Warren stopped well short of where the teacher wanted him to sit. He changed direction and rowed back to a position directly opposite the room.

There were bits of Warren that reminded Jamie of herself, a couple of years ago. Not so much the kicking and punching, but all the snarling and the mouthing off.

Things had changed a bit. She hadn't even thought about looking into the classroom. There was a time when she couldn't have stopped herself.

If only she could keep the picture of herself in her mind. Concentrate on what she wanted to be. The trouble was that she still lost it sometimes. Everything became a blur until she calmed down.

Warren rowed back to the starting line. He leaned towards the ventilation grill in the bottom of the door and made farting noises into the room.

Jamie stood up. She'd decided to apologise, but there was no way she was writing a stupid letter.

Every time I come back to my office there's more paperwork on the desk.

BEHAVIOUR REPORT	
Student: Alex Marlow (I think)	
Teacher: Terry Spear	**Lesson/Time:** L3/12:10
Subject/Location: Maths/Outside Room 13	

Description of incident, including attempts to prevent or change student behaviour:

There was a student riding his bike outside my room in Lesson 4. He came over, looked in the room and started pressing his face against the window – sticking his tongue out. I went to open the window and speak to him, but he gave everyone the finger and raced off down Lachlan Terrace. The kids told me his name was Alex Marlow. Apparently he's a new Year 8 but he hasn't been here yet.

I checked with the principal and the front office to see what the latest was on enrolled Year 8s who hadn't arrived. The home phone had been disconnected. The feeder primary school didn't know anything new. They said his attendance was poor and he was a behaviour problem when he was in school. A home visit was on Angela Davis' list, but she'd been too busy to get to it. I'd have to follow up myself.

'Mrs Marlow?'

'Yeah.' A suspicious voice came out from behind the broken flywire.

'I'm Craig Eliot. I'm the Deputy Principal at Southside High School.'

'What d'you want? Is it about Alex?'

'Yes.'

The screen door pushed open. Mrs Marlow was obviously about to go out – she was wearing high heels, a short black skirt and sunglasses. A small boy followed close behind.

'That's it! If he's in more trouble he's going straight back to his dad. He told me he won a prize yesterday for good behaviour – a basketball cap.'

'Well, there seems to be a problem here,' I said, 'because Alex hasn't been to school this week. He hasn't been inside the buildings, at any rate.'

'The little shit! That's it. I can't put up with this any more. His dad can have him, and welcome.'

I wasn't sure what to say. The issue had suddenly become bigger than checking on a Year 8 enrolment.

'You little shit!' Mrs Marlow was yelling down the road.

A young boy on a BMX skidded to a halt at the corner. He stared towards us, adjusting his cap.

'Don't think you're coming back here for lunch. Won a prize for good behaviour, did you? I'll give you a prize for good behaviour!'

She raised her hand and stepped towards him. Then her hands fell to her sides. She was close to tears.

Alex swung his bike round and headed back the way he'd come. The small child had started crying. He was clinging to his mother's leg.

'Be quiet,' she insisted, 'or I'll send you to school.'

The child stopped crying immediately. His mother sat down on the porch step, lifted him onto her lap and hugged him.

There was a silence before I spoke.

'I know it's a bit of a pain, but if we don't see Alex in the next few days we'll have to let the attendance people know.'

There was another silence. Then, with her face still buried in the child's hair, she said, 'He won't be here. I'm sending him back to his dad.'

'We've got a female counsellor at the school. If you'd like to see her, I can arrange it,' I offered.

As I listened to my own words, I wondered how much work

Angela could take on, and how much she could do anyway. There didn't seem to be any limit to the problems I was seeing.

I dashed home tonight to go to a movie with Nicole. Her mother had agreed to babysit the kids. I stopped what I was doing at four-fifteen and walked out.

I needed to do some marking, but it would have to wait.

'I'm home!' I wanted every second of my presence to be noticed.

'We're in the bathroom.'

'Daddy!' Marc beamed and reached out with both arms.

'Da, da.' Renae splashed the surface of the water with her pudgy little hands.

Nicole crouched by the bath, sponging Renae. 'I've still got to get ready. Can you finish bathing the kids and get them into bed?'

As soon as she'd gone, I lifted Renae out of the water, wrapped her in a towel and quickly fetched my diary and mobile phone. I needed two relief teachers for the next day.

I sat on the edge of the bath, with Renae on my lap, and looked up the numbers. Marc grabbed the top of the diary to see what I was doing. Water dribbled off his hand and rolled in fat smudges down the page.

'No!' I pulled back sharply.

The top of the page peeled away in his hand. His face quivered and he burst into tears.

'Sorry, Marc. Daddy didn't mean to shout.'

I dropped the diary on the floor and gathered him up.

'What on earth's going on?' Nicole reappeared with another towel. 'What are you doing?'

'I had a couple of phone calls to make.'

Nicole turned away. I decided to make any future work calls from the toilet.

Marc's crying subsided. There was a knock at the door.

'That'll be Mum,' said Nicole.

We both looked at the open diary on the tiles. Blotches were spread across the page like a fungus, smearing names and numbers together.

Nicole reached down, closed the diary and handed it to me. 'You'd better let her in and make those calls. I'll take over here.' There was a pause before she added, 'If you're quick, you'll get it done before the pages stick together.'

'We'll go to a movie then get a gourmet pizza at Cafe Palermo.' Paula was making suggestions for Jamie's birthday. 'They've got an outside balcony with umbrellas.'

'Costs more,' said Ricky.

Paula glared at him.

'They do great pizzas, though,' he added quickly.

'It's better than getting takeaway and watching videos at my place,' Paula insisted. They'd discussed having a party, but Jamie didn't want one. It was too difficult, working out who to ask and who to leave out. Then there were the gate-crashers and idiots who thought party was spelt p..u..k..e, but never cleaned up.

'I'll get Dominic to come,' said Ricky enthusiastically. 'He's got a full-time job now. He's rolling in money.'

Jamie couldn't suppress a spark of interest at the mention of Dominic's name.

'Do you think Dominic will want to come?'

Ricky flicked the butt of his cigarette towards a small sand-tray as they wandered into the Mall. It went in. 'Yeah! Woah! Thank you, thank you.' He raised his arms triumphantly to acknowledge the imaginary crowd.

'What about Dominic?' Jamie repeated.

'Ask him yourself,' said Ricky. 'I'm meeting him here in two minutes.'

'Can you come?' *Don't look too excited. Keep still.*

'Yes. You'll have to let me buy you a birthday drink.'

Dominic looked calm. His chest couldn't be churning like an eggbeater, as hers was.

'I've got a new job.'

'Ricky told me.'

'At a meat-processing factory, making hamburger mixes. I do early shifts now, so I can make the movie easy.'

Great! Everything was falling into place.

'I don't want to stay at Ricky's much longer. It's crowded enough with his brother and sisters.'

She nodded. At least with Pat she had some space to herself.

'Soon I'll be able to manage on my own.'

Jamie wanted to ask what he meant exactly by *managing on his own*.

Another time. The question might sound naive. She wanted to seem mature.

Her new dark eyeliner and subtle make-up helped.

It was only Pat who hadn't noticed that she'd grown up. Pat thought being grown-up meant using buckets of make-up. She put it on with a trowel and used a blowtorch to get it off.

'Hey! Dom. Check this out.' The shout was so loud, nearly everybody in the Mall turned round. Ricky was beckoning frantically from just inside the entrance.

Ricky and Kane peered at the engine as Anton stomped on the accelerator. Each burst of noise produced grins of approval. Dominic hung back, either less curious or less impressed.

'It's Anton,' she explained. The bellowing engine nearly drowned her voice.

Jamie cupped a hand to her mouth. 'He goes to our school. Repeating Year 12.'

Anton unfolded himself from the car and dropped the hood.

Ricky and Kane knelt down to check out the exhaust. They circled the car admiringly, kicking tyres and tapping the bodywork.

Jamie read the badge on the boot – Mazda. It was blue, with black vinyl seats and tinted windows.

Alex Marlow appeared from nowhere.

'Crock o' shit,' he grinned.

'Watch him,' warned Ricky. 'He'll nick your stereo.'

'Where do you think I got it from?' said Anton. He reached in and cranked up the sound for a few seconds. The whole car shuddered as the bass reverberated through the panels.

'Wanna a lift?'

Ricky dived into the front seat. Jamie motioned Dominic into the back and scrambled in after him. Paula and Kane squeezed in the other side.

Struggling to buckle her seatbelt, Jamie jammed her hand between Dominic and herself. Dominic's hand covered her own and took hold of the belt clip. He leaned across her, pulled out more belt and clicked it in place.

Tyres squealing, they spurted towards the exit, signalling left. Alex jumped back, dragging his bike with him.

'Other way!' yelled Jamie. 'Go to my place.'

'Why?'

'Just do it. It's clear behind.' It was the chance she'd been waiting for. *Get Pat.*

The car swerved into the central slip-lane. Jamie was forced into the corner as they were all thrown off balance. Then bodies pressed together, and Dominic's dreadlocks brushed her face. He braced his arm against the window.

'Take it easy, mate. We're not all belted in,' he growled.

Anton tapped the accelerator, like an edgy smoker.

They darted in front of a delivery truck and onto the round-about, to shrieks and giggles from Paula and Kane. Dominic couldn't stay upright. Jamie was smothered again.

'Shit!' The stab of fear was uncontrollable as the car lurched from side to side.

'Are you deaf, dickhead?' Dominic was angry. He was jabbing Anton's shoulder.

They drew up outside Pat's place.

'No worries,' grinned Anton. 'I'll gun it as soon as she comes out.'

Jamie ran to the house. She tapped the window and thumped the door with the side of her fist.

Pat would go crazy. Good.

As she dashed back to the car, the boys tumbled out.

'He's doin' a stand-still,' said Ricky. 'We're liftin' the back. Get in.'

Jamie grabbed the back bumper alongside Ricky and Kane.

'Keep the revs up,' yelled Ricky.

Pat's face appeared round the side of the door. It was like a green light at a Grand Prix.

'Li i i i ft!' Ricky's voice thinned as he took the strain.

The body rose on the springs as they heaved together.

'Dump the clutch! Dump it!'

The tyres whipped over the bitumen, spitting out rubber and grit. Kane swore as a burst of hot exhaust gas hit his legs.

Pat glared, mouth set, arms folded tight.

Vibrations shuddered through Jamie's arms, into her body.

'Ready?' shouted Ricky.

'Let go!'

Rubber ripped into the road.

Jamie winced. Acrid smoke irritated her nostrils and caught in her throat. The screeching noise doubled. She instinctively covered her ears.

For the first time she realised that Dominic was out of the car and walking away. He was well past Alex Marlow, who had caught up with them on his bike.

The car rocketed to the right, engraving dark black lines on the road, and bounced over the kerb. It clunked and scraped viciously along the fence towards Alex. The driver's wing mirror smashed against a fencepost, spraying shattered glass and plastic into the air.

Alex disappeared from sight.

Jamie raced to catch up, feeling sick.

Anton looked deathly pale. Glass spilled to the ground as he emerged from the passenger door.

Alex was sitting, holding his elbow. Jamie breathed more easily.

Blood trickled from his arm. He stared silently at his bike. The twisted front wheel was wedged under the car tyre, and the handlebars were rammed crookedly against the gatepost.

Dominic had sprinted back. He was staring at her, then his gaze shifted to Anton.

'Good one, mate. You're a real legend.'

Jamie looked at him. 'If there's something you want to say to me, just say it.'

Dominic shook his head and walked away.

Jamie looked back at Pat. She was gloating. The way she was standing, the tilt of her head – even from this distance you could tell.

Jamie wanted to scream.

I took Jamie Joel into my English lesson today. She'd forgotten her consent form for ten-pin bowling. Rather than let her socialise in the library, I told her to come with me.

It wasn't what she expected. Being with Year 9s was an embarrassment. Her pursed lips and resentful expression suggested she'd be better organised next time.

'What's *she* doin' here?' piped up Jarrad Hardie.

Jamie's ferocious glare convinced him to look away.

I moved a couple of students and sat Jamie on her own.

'Have you got something to get on with, or would you like me to give you work?'

'I've got something,' she responded icily, and rummaged through her bag.

'You should all have your work out by now. Bags on the floor, please.' I reminded the class. 'The books from the library are on the cabinet. If anyone wants to use lyrics from the songs we heard last lesson, there are photocopies on my desk.'

Several students handed me copies of lyrics and CDs to be played later in the lesson.

'This'll give you a headache,' Jarrad grinned.

'As long as it's not a heart attack,' I replied.

'Track 7 would do that. It's full of dirty words.'

'It's like you, then,' someone muttered.

Laughter rippled through the room.

Jamie had a weighty-looking Maths book open on her desk.

I'd flipped through her file after our first meeting and been surprised by the high exam results. Incomplete coursework usually brought her grades down. She had the potential to do better than she was doing.

She leaned across and whispered to Ashlee Sinclair, passing her a folded piece of paper.

I quietly meandered to the back of the room.

'How's it going, Ashlee?'

'Good.'

'Anything I can help you with?'

She shook her head.

'Would you like me to check Jamie's writing for you?'

Jamie's arm shot out like a lizard's tongue and whisked it off the desk.

I couldn't help laughing.

'So what is it you don't want me to see?'

'Nothing.'

'Show him, Jamie. It's great!'

Jamie pushed the sheet deep into her bag.

'It's a poem,' offered Ashlee excitedly. 'It's about this real hunk with dreadlocks and . . .'

The flash of annoyance told her she'd said too much.

I gave Jamie time to settle down before speaking.

'Do you write much poetry?'

'Sometimes.'

'The kids here are going to spiral-bind their work into books with protective plastic covers,' I explained. 'If you ever want to make your poems into a book, let me know. I'll show you how to do it . . . it makes important things look really special.'

'Thanks,' she responded warily.

She was right to be suspicious. I wasn't sure that the incident with Jessica Rowan had been properly resolved. It was on my list of things to find out.

Jason and Shaun, the bottle recyclers, seem to enjoy being on attendance cards. Jason has even turned it to his advantage with his mother.

'I did well yesterday, didn't I?' he said, pointing to the teachers' initials indicating he'd attended every lesson.

'When do we stop doing it?' asked Shaun.

'A week supervised by me. Another two weeks supervised by your home-group teacher. Then, if there are no problems, you can carry on as normal. But,' I emphasised, looking at them closely, 'I'll be putting out a special note to your teachers asking them to let me know the minute either one of you is missing.'

'I want to keep doing it,' said Jason. 'Mum said she'd buy me a McDonald's every week it's filled in properly.'

Every day is another frenetic succession of events. Things keep coming at me from all directions. It's like being in front of several tennis ball machines at once. They're all firing at maximum speed, but for some reason or other I've only been equipped with a table tennis bat.

It's no wonder half the clocks around the school don't work. Kane Brock was sent to me today for taking batteries for his CD player. He said he was buying them cheap from someone else until he realised where they came from.

The glass repairman stormed into my office in a foul temper this morning. Someone had lobbed a rock at his truck and smashed several panes of glass before they could be used to replace the broken windows.

Three ex-students came into the yard at lunchtime. They said they wanted to speak to someone, but wouldn't say who it was. It didn't look like a social call. One of them had a baseball bat.

Leon Ducoski, the sports teacher, handed me this letter from Mrs Kelland. He thought it might be best if I dealt with her.

Dear Mr Ducoski

No way is Nick wearing different bloody clothes after doing PE lessons and here are the reasons.

1. I am not giving him more clothes to make my washing pile bigger.
2. the lessons are not long enough to build up a good sweat.
3. let them have a bloody shower after the lessons to stop the stink
4. do you change YOUR clothes after EACH LESSON

So don't give him any more bloody bullshit work to do and don't keep him in

from
L Kelland
If you still have a problem the school's got my phone number

'I'm going out with Paula and Ricky.' Jamie spoke over the noise of the TV.

'You are, are you?' Pat's tone was acid.

A surge of irritation pushed Jamie forward in her seat. 'What do you mean?' Already it was hard to keep the peace.

'It's not just Ricky and Paula you're going out with, is it?' Pat looked at her for the first time. 'How come you haven't mentioned the other person?'

'Dominic?' Jamie was partly thinking aloud. 'D'you mean Dominic?'

'So that's his name. Nice of you to mention it.'

Suddenly it all made sense.

'It's Debbie, isn't it? She saw us when she was shopping. She's been blabbing on the phone.'

Pat looked away momentarily.

'What's she been saying?' Jamie's lips curled resentfully. 'Or what's she been making up, more like? Bitch!'

'Don't you talk about Deb like that,' Pat fumed. 'She only said what she saw.' Pat was red in the face under her make-up. 'I saw him as well, by the car the other day, him with the hair like dead cats' tails. . . . And you needn't look like that, because if it was all so innocent you wouldn't be trying to keep it a secret.'

'You're sick, you are. D'you know that?' exclaimed Jamie bitterly.

Musical chimes sounded in the hallway. Pat huffed her way to the front door.

'It's for you,' she called out abruptly.

The sight of Paula, Ricky and Dominic crowding the doorstep caught Jamie by surprise. She shouldered Pat aside to join them as they retreated down the path.

'We brought you something to open in the morning,' said Paula, holding out three brightly coloured envelopes, obviously birthday cards. 'What's up?'

Jamie glanced towards the house. Pat was still blocking the doorway.

Jamie flung her arms around Dominic and kissed him passionately on the mouth.

Before he could speak, she took hold of his hand and led him away.

'Put your arm round me,' she hissed, slipping her hand round his waist. 'Don't look back.' She didn't want Pat to see Dominic's bewildered expression. 'And don't get any ideas either.'

Jamie had trouble concentrating in class. She'd avoided Pat by staying out late, then getting up early. She kept going over things in her mind.

'It was Pat, crappin' on about you – going mental.' She didn't want Dominic thinking she was a deranged slut. 'I knew it would get right up her nose.'

He shrugged.

'I don't usually jump on boys,' she insisted.

'Any time – feel free.' The corners of Dominic's mouth creased slightly.

She flicked his dreadlocks.

Still couldn't believe she'd done it. Acted on impulse. Stomped on Jamie cam'.

It felt like two minutes ago. The smooth texture of his lips as she coaxed them apart. The tingle through her body as she hugged him.

He'd been good about it after she explained. He didn't use it against her, or make suggestive comments, the way some boys would have.

Perhaps he was thinking them. Perhaps he was waiting for his luck to kick in again.

She longed to know what *he* felt when they kissed, when their bodies touched.

He did ask about the latest bust-up with Pat, and what she was going to do about it. And he told her how things went wrong with his stepdad.

'Never liked him,' said Dominic. 'It was okay when he first moved in. Then he started acting like he owned the place.'

'Too hands-on,' Jamie sympathised.

Dominic smiled, recognising his own words. 'He's a gorilla.'

Jamie giggled.

'Honest. He's as hairy as.'

'What happened to your real dad?'

'Workplace accident – long time ago. It wasn't his fault.' Things went quiet between them.

Dominic would be a good friend, like Ricky, but more grown-up. Like the birthday cards really.

Paula's card had a cute kitten on the front and a printed rhyme about everyone being special. Dominic's was a simple hand-written 'Happy Birthday'. Ricky had scribbled 'Good eh?'. His card was rude.

Books slap closed. Chairs scrape.

Recess.

Not much room for books in her bag. It was full of clothes. She was sleeping at Paula's.

Sharleen brought Cathy Lee to the staff meeting last night. Sharleen gave a report on the canteen, then told new staff about the Breakfast Program.

Mrs Lee announced that she'd offered to help out and would gradually take over the running of the program.

I made a note to drop in one morning, when things weren't quite so busy.

I was sitting next to Greg Proden. He asked if it was true about me making a home visit to chase up a Year 8 truant called Marlow.

'Yes, why?'

'Don't know why you bother,' said Greg, 'We're better off without kids like that.'

'We've got a legal obligation to contact the home,' I replied, trying not to get drawn in. 'And they're not on the phone.'

'Send a letter. That's what Strehborn would have done.'

I tried not to look irritated.

'It works a treat,' he added. 'It covers the school, and there's less chance the kid'll turn up, because most of the people round here can't read.'

Next time, if the only vacant seat is next to Greg, I'll stand.

I got up early this morning and started some marking.

Jarrad Hardie has problems with copying titles, let alone spelling, but he's not short of unusual ideas.

> *Life would be much more intresting if peeple could fly*
> *I disgree that it would be better if peeple could fly cause someone*
> *mite think I was a duck and I'd get shot.*

Most kids revel in possibilities such as flying over skyscrapers, avoiding traffic jams and going on holidays overseas without having to pay airfares.

Jarrad had a different line of thought altogether. He said that he'd need a suit that changed colours to match the sky, so that people couldn't see him. It would be great for breaking into houses and stealing from shops. And if he robbed a bank he wouldn't need a getaway car.

He finished by saying that if he got caught and sent to prison, he'd fly away when he was in the exercise yard, and he'd stay down low, to avoid the duck shooters.

I'm out at a conference today. The principal was keen for me to go.

Unfortunately, the relief teacher I've booked is new to the school. No one else was available. The kids have a reputation for giving relief teachers a hard time unless they've really got their act together.

My desk will be covered in paperwork when I get back and I'll probably have to follow up on discipline. It'll take me a week to catch up.

The best thing is that I'll get to finish my coffees during the day and I won't get dragged away at lunchtime to deal with kids who've caused trouble in the yard.

That's definitely something to look forward to.

The smell of smoke in the girls' toilets was strong, but no one was there. The cubicle doors were all open.

Jamie lit a cigarette, dumped her bag on a toilet seat and leaned against the dividing wall, ready to shut the door if anyone came in.

If it was a teacher, she'd stick the lighter in her knickers and flush the cigarette down the toilet. She'd say the smoke was there when she arrived.

F--k Proden. No way she'd go to the withdrawal room.

He'd picked on her as soon as she walked in the room. Once a prick always a prick.

'Homework assignments are due today. Put them on my desk as you come in. . . . Forgotten something, have we, Miss Joel? Life's too busy to remember deadlines, is it?'

Don't bite back. The assignment was three-quarters done. *Ask for an extension later.* If she asked now he'd rub her face in it, in front of the class.

Other kids were walking straight to their desks. It wasn't just her.

'You do realise that simply attending lessons is not enough?'

'You're full of crap, you are.' She couldn't stop herself.

Footsteps.

Jamie stubbed out the cigarette and closed the cubicle door.

More footsteps. Two people.

'What kept ya?'

'Contaris was explaining stuff to the whole class. She wouldn't let me go till she'd finished.'

More footsteps.

'About time! We thought you weren't coming.'

Jamie didn't recognise the voices, but she knew the routine. Friends asking to go to the toilet at the same time for a smoke. Quick pee – slow fag – peppermint spray and back to class.

Someone rattled the door of Jamie's cubicle.

'Who's in there?'

'Piss off!'

Jamie didn't bother re-lighting her cigarette. With three of them puffing away she'd be able to smoke passively for the rest of the lesson.

Her thoughts shifted to Cafe Palermo. Her birthday had been great.

'You can have any drink you like. I can afford it,' Dominic assured her. 'I was promoted after three days.'

'That's brilliant!'

'Not when all the others are morons,' Ricky chipped in.

'And you'd know about that, wouldn't you?' laughed Paula.

'I'm moving into a caravan at the weekend,' said Dominic.

'Sweet – get m'room to m'self again,' spluttered Ricky, his mouth slopping with Coke and half-chewed pizza.

'It's happened quicker than I planned,' Dominic confided quietly.

Jamie beamed. She was pleased for him, but she wished *she* had a plan – a way of escaping Pat.

I'll have to show Mel Richter's writing to Angela Davis. It looks like more counselling work for Angela and a confidential notification to the authorities. I'd like to think Mel's work is pure fiction. Something tells me it's not.

In class, we talked about letters to newspaper editors or the school council. The topics the students came up with ranged from school uniform and homework to pollution and community attitudes towards young people. But Mel had more pressing issues.

Letter to Mum and Dad

Dear Mum and Dad,

I have something I want to say and I'm writing it in a letter because I'm scared to say it to your face.

I hate it when you fight all the time over stupid things. I know that me and Ryan fight but we don't tear the family apart. You make me so upset I just feel like running away and Ryan wants to come too. We can't stand all the yelling, hitting and throwing.

Dad, this bit is for you. Even after the Restraining Order you haven't been any better. You shouldn't have stopped going to the counselling classes they told you to go to.

Now for Mum, don't pretend it's just Dad because you get all nasty too.

Do you remember the time when you said that I could talk to you about anything? It doesn't work because everyone gets mad. That's why I'm thinking of running away. I wouldn't be writing this letter if what you said was true.

Mel.

I finally caught up with Jessica Rowan to see what had happened about Jamie Joel. I can't believe that it's taken me over a week to get back to her.

It wasn't resolved. Jamie was working on a desk outside the classroom.

'I don't see why I should be in trouble in the first place for just reading something out.'

'If I stood at the front of the school assembly, introduced the next speaker, then read out "something" because someone had graffitied the lectern, do you think it would be acceptable?'

Jamie couldn't prevent the hint of a smile.

'You don't have to say anything, Jamie. You and I both know that what you said was unacceptable, and that's why there needs to be a written apology and a detention. As far as I'm concerned, Mrs Rowan is being incredibly fair in giving you the benefit of the doubt. If it happens again it'll be a suspension.'

Jamie was still for a moment before she spoke.

'Okay, I'll write an apology and do the detention. Can I go back to class now?'

I was taken aback. I turned to Jessica Rowan.

'Is there anything you want to say?'

She was about to speak when there was a knock at the door. Greg Proden looked in.

Jamie slumped back in her chair.

'Could I have a quick word?'

I moved to the doorway. He kept his voice low.

'I just wanted to check that you had all the details about the incident at the start of my lesson yesterday. She claimed what she said was written on her desk and she was just reading it out . . .'

He paused when he saw me shake my head.

'Come in,' I said, 'You'd better join us.'

There was no reply when I phoned Jamie's aunt to inform her about the suspension, so I handed Jamie an envelope with the paperwork to take home.

'Will Mrs Reynolds be in tonight?'

'Dunno.'

'Well, I'll ring again later. Then I can answer any questions she might have.'

'She won't care.'

Jamie shoved the letter into her bag.

'I'll see you on Wednesday morning for the re-entry meeting. Come prepared to make a fresh start.'

Jamie wasn't ready for fresh starts. She wanted to see something obnoxious written on a desk that she could read to me.

It was all over. Might as well leave school. Nothing ever worked out.

Jamie kicked her way through the long grass on the edge of the oval. She'd already ripped open the envelope and read the letter, starting *Regrettably I have to inform you* . . .

Regrettably! What a heap of shit. They just wrote that to make it sound as if they cared. The deputy had been after her ever since he'd seen her in the corridor that first time. And Proden couldn't have been happier. His main problem was trying not to look too pleased.

The official form had *Notice Of Suspension From School* in large print across the top. It had the dates of the suspension on it and said Jamie couldn't go back to normal classes unless a parent or guardian came in for a meeting. That meant Pat.

If Pat didn't make the meeting, Jamie would be stuck somewhere else doing her work until the meeting took place. Kids were usually put in a small room in the office area. You couldn't even have recess and lunch with everybody else.

Stuff that!

She pulled the suspension papers out of her bag, tore them into little pieces and threw them in the bin by the bus stop. The envelope followed, in a crumpled ball.

Pat didn't need to find out yet. It could wait.

Jamie dumped her bag just inside the front door, where she wouldn't forget it. She'd be out of the house when Pat came back from Friday shopping with Debbie. Then she'd come in again, carrying her school bag, as if the day had been normal.

It was impossible to just sit and watch TV. She found a pen and some paper. There was a saying on a desk calendar she'd always remembered: 'Every day is the first day of the rest of your life'. It made her feel better when things were in a mess. She could put everything behind her and make a new start.

The last new start had been the plan to go back to school and stay out of trouble. It was time to start again, with a list of places where she could apply for a job.

She could talk to Dominic. He'd help her out.

The phone rang. Probably the deputy. Ignore it.

She scribbled *phone* on a piece of paper and put it next to her bag. It was a reminder to disconnect the phone before she left, so the deputy couldn't speak to Pat.

Warren Horrowitz's name came up in a student support meeting today. It involved Aaron Lee as well.

During Tech. Studies, Aaron had used the drill press to drill a hole through the middle of Warren's school diary. Warren had asked him to do it. That didn't make it acceptable, but the main problem was that someone had put the teacher's diary underneath Warren's diary and now there was a twelve-millimetre hole in both of them.

Warren denied knowing anything about the teacher's diary and Aaron accepted the blame, but insisted that he didn't know how it got there.

Gary Hawthorne had given his diary to someone to bring

to the meeting so we could see the damage. But that wasn't the point of the meetings. They were intended to decide strategies to help particular students in need of support.

In this case, Aaron was the student needing support. Apparently it wasn't the first time Warren had set him up.

Alex Marlow was seen hanging around the school again, on his bike. He was at the edge of the oval, watching kids playing football in PE. The teacher also mentioned that one of the footballs went missing.

I made a confidential report this morning on the hotline that deals with suspected abuse. Mel Richter came to school with a nasty scratch down her arm. She said her father did it with a bottle cap. I also made her an appointment with Angela Davis to see if there was anything else that we could do.

Nick Kelland was reported by the yard duty teacher for hitting a girl. When I spoke to him he was quite distressed. He said that Ashlee Sinclair was in love with him and she wouldn't stop pestering him to go out with her. He said he'd told several teachers but they didn't do anything. They just laughed. He said he knew he shouldn't have done it, but he didn't want to apologise or he'd never get rid of her again.

I need to speak to Jason Gillet and Shaun Neale. Their names top the list of suspects following two related incidents this afternoon. All the hens' eggs disappeared during Year 9 Agriculture. Most of them were discovered again after school. They were on Gary Hawthorne's car.

This job's always in your head. There are things that need following up even if it is Saturday.

'Is that Mrs Reynolds?'

'Yes.'

'This is Craig Eliot here, from Southside High School. I'm the new deputy. I've phoned to talk about Jamie. I rang last night but I couldn't get a reply. Did she tell you she was suspended yesterday?'

'The little cow!' I moved the phone away from my ear.

'Jamie? Jamie?'

The voice echoed down the phone. Doors opening and closing, feet clumping away, then returning.

'She's not here. I'll kill her when I catch her.'

'Do you need to call the police?'

'Only if they can lock her up.'

'I hope you find her. She can come back Wednesday, but you need to come with her.' I hurried the last words. She seemed keen to get off the phone.

'Waste of time. Lying little bitch.' She hung up.

I stood by the phone a second, contemplating the world at the other end of the line. I decided I'd ring back Monday morning.

'If I go home, I'll fuckin' kill her. Then she'll wish she kept her big nose out of it. . . . She's got no right. She's not even my mother.' Jamie sat hunched on the edge of the bed, close to tears. Paula put an arm round her.

Pat had phoned and Mrs Fiorito said Jamie had to go home.

'I'm not going.'

'Don't worry about it. We'll sort something out.'

'She can't force me,' insisted Jamie. 'I bet she just wants to stuff it up for me so I can't stay here.' She started packing her belongings. 'I'll sleep in a bus shelter.' Looking up, she caught

Paula's eye. 'I'll nick a shopping trolley and push all my gear around in that.'

Laughter. Her anger began to subside. Jamie cam'. More things came into focus.

She wouldn't be the first if she went for the bus shelter. Samantha Heures slept rough after bust-ups with her dad. But the close-up Jamie had of herself sleeping out was frightening. It gave her a sick chill in her chest and stomach. She'd be on the streets, after dark, with all the druggies, psychos and ferals. Anyway, she wouldn't do it for long.

Jamie tightened the drawstring on her bag, pulled the flap over and clicked it in place. 'Let's go. I'll tell your mum it's a misunderstanding: I left a note but Pat didn't see it.'

'Where are we going?'

'The bus stop down the end of the road. I'll start putting my things out, ready for tonight.' She made out that it was a joke, but the sick feeling was still there, gnawing away inside her.

I saw Jamie when I was shopping with Nicole and the children this morning. She was with Ricky Whan and a girl whose name I don't know. Last year, if we went to Southside Mall I didn't know anyone, and no one knew me. Now I recognise students all the time.

I was relieved to see that Jamie was safe.

'Wait here a second. I've seen someone I've got to speak to quickly.' Nicole looked at me quizzically as Marc tugged her arm and pointed to a coin-in-the-slot helicopter outside the supermarket.

Jamie spotted me. She halted, then started to turn away. I hurried towards her, before she could walk off.

'Hello. I'm glad to see you're okay.'

She wasn't slow. She realised that I'd spoken to Mrs Reynolds.

'Why wouldn't I be?'

I ignored the question.

'So I'll see you on Wednesday, then?' I tried to sound encouraging, concerned about her future.

'Are they your kids?'

'Yes.' I turned to Nicole, who was coming up behind me. Jamie looked at her blankly, before speaking to me again.

'I think you're needed,' she said. 'You'd better go.'

'So Wednesday, then?' It was worth one more try.

Jamie shrugged, without giving eye contact, and walked away.

'How rude was that?' Nicole exclaimed.

'Come on. Let's keep going,' I said, spinning the rattle on the front of the pusher and whisking Marc onto my shoulders.

'It's more complicated than it seems,' I added, by way of explanation. 'She's got a few problems at the minute.'

'She's not the only one,' answered Nicole. 'Most families can relax when they go shopping.'

'I'll organise a party at my place, then you can sleep over.' Ricky fanned spiralling smoke away from his face.

A beeping truck reversed past them, into a delivery bay at the back of the Mall.

'I'll tell Mum we're getting takeaway and a stack of videos,' continued Ricky. 'We'll crash in the rumpus room.'

'She won't let you,' said Paula. She mimicked his mother's voice: *"You should have thought of it sooner."'*

Paula's comments sank in.

Jamie stared at the ground. Point number one, she wasn't going home tonight. Point number two, she wasn't going home tomorrow. Nothing Pat did was going to make her go back.

'Yeah! Woah! Thank you, thank you.' Ricky was on his feet, arms raised. 'I've got it!'

'You've had it ever since I've known you,' said Paula.

Ricky ignored her. 'Go on then, ask me what it is.'

'What is it?' Jamie obliged.

'I'll tell Mum it's a farewell party for Dominic. She can't say no to that. She said herself we should have done something.'

'Will she let us sleep over?'

He flashed them a grin. 'I'll tell her Dominic can't make it till later tonight, so it'll be best if people stay.' He paused to get the details clear in his own mind. 'Dominic's fetching some stuff for the caravan this afternoon. I'll get to him first, so he knows what to say.'

Jamie gave him a hug. 'Thanks.'

Ricky looked embarrassed. He was more at ease with the adulation of his imaginary crowd. He broke into a run, side-stepped a mother with a pusher, and darted into the Mall.

Paula grabbed Jamie's arm. 'Let's get something to eat.'

'Good idea,' Jamie agreed.

'But there's something else I want to do first.'

'Think he'll like it?'

'Of course he will. How many times are you going to ask?'

Paula didn't understand. She thought it was a simple matter of having the hots for Dominic. Why else go to the trouble of a card and present?

It was impossible to explain without offending her.

Dominic *had* to like the present. It was a perfect match for his dragon pendant – a small pewter wizard with a raised staff in one hand. His other arm was outstretched, holding a crystal ball.

Dominic would look at the crystal ball and wonder what lay ahead. She knew he would. She'd looked at it herself, and wondered the same thing.

A familiar figure appeared, silhouetted against the entrance to the Mall: Ricky. The swagger in his step was gone and he wouldn't hold Jamie's gaze.

The sick feeling rose from her stomach to her throat.

'She wouldn't let us sleep over, would she?' said Paula, before Ricky could speak.

'Pat phoned. She's phoning everyone and giving them all that shit about you having to go home and not being allowed to sleep over.'

Jamie suppressed the urge to ring Pat and blast her before she could put down the phone. 'Is Dominic coming here?' There was urgency in Jamie's voice.

'She's got a present for him,' Paula explained. 'She took a *long* time choosing it.'

'I *see*,' Ricky emphasised.

'You don't see anything,' snapped Jamie. 'Is he coming or not?'

'He'll be at the Rec. Centre at six.'

Jamie looked at her watch. Two hours to kill.

'What about tonight?' asked Paula. 'Where will you stay?'

That was Jamie's question exactly.

I've just checked the folder I left for the relief teacher, while I was at the conference. The lesson was a shambles.

Seven boys left twenty minutes early for sports practice. Apparently they had a note signed by another teacher. It must have been forged, but even if the reliever was suspicious, he was probably pleased to see them go.

I've got a list as long as my arm of kids to follow up, with things like refusing to sit where requested, swearing, snapping pencils and walking across desks to get to the front of the class.

It sounds as if he started shouting as soon as he got in the room.

The lion-tamer approach rarely works. It can encourage kids to take you on.

I can see from the worksheets, that very little was done. The teacher wrote more than the students. His notes reminded me of my conversation with Jarrad Hardie. When I saw him in the yard and asked if he'd completed all the work I'd set for the relief lesson, he said, 'No, but it was the teacher's fault'. He insisted that the teacher kept telling the class to stop working.

'Jarrad, teachers don't spend their time telling kids to stop working.'

'This one did. He even yelled it out a few times.'

'Can you remember the exact words he said?'

'Yeah.'

'What were they?'

'He kept saying, "Stop what you're doing and listen to me".'

Jamie's whole body was tense.

Creaking, scratching. Rats? Should she yell for help?

She tried to tell herself that the noises were outside. Leaves rustling, skittering across the path. Branches creaking in the wind. A cat scrambling up a fence.

She was still in control. Pat would never get another chance to gloat.

The image of Pat transformed into a stalker staring at her through night-vision goggles.

She leant out and swept her arm in an arc, alongside the mattress.

No one there. She rolled back into the warm spot.

Still, this was better than a bus stop. She was surrounded by old junk, but at least the shed had four walls. She'd ask Paula for a torch in the morning. And a CD player, to drown out the creepy noises. Perhaps a knife as well.

Her biggest worry was going to the toilet in the dark. She'd have to hold on and dash out for a pee as soon as it was light.

It was good that she hadn't had to ask Dominic if she could stay in his caravan. In the Mall or the Rec. Centre, Dominic was a friend. Locked away in a caravan, he might be different. She was still getting to know him.

Dominic really liked the wizard.

'Cool. It's like a picture I had on the wall once.' He gave her a hug – spontaneous, grateful.

'I liked it better than the dragons,' she admitted.

'It's great! A bit different to the things Ricky's mum gave me.'

'What?'

'Packets of noodles and toilet rolls,' he laughed.

Jamie tried to imagine the wizard on display.

She pictured a Hollywood trailer with a suite of rooms and a spa. No – more likely a beat-up little dogbox with a shabby curtain divider.

She liked the beat-up dogbox best. The wizard stood out more. The crystal ball sparkled against the dull surrounds.

When I checked my diary for next week I wondered about submitting some new names to the student support group. I don't know what gets into some kids. You never know what they'll do next, but you can rely on the fact that it'll be crazy.

There has been a spate of ruler thefts around the school. It had been going on for a while, but nobody really noticed.

It was brought to my attention last week after Jason Gillet and Shaun Neale complained to their teacher, saying that their rulers had been stolen and equipment wasn't safe in the school. On inquiring, the teacher found that over half of the students in the class claimed to have lost a ruler in the past two or three weeks. The same was true for the students in surrounding classes.

I told the kids to keep their eyes open and to let me know if they had any suspicions.

Two lessons later, Jason and Shaun came to see me with several students whose rulers had been taken while they were in PE.

I asked them to go through their bags carefully, in front of me, to make sure there had been no mistake.

Some days you get lucky. There was something about the way that Jason lifted his bag and slid it over his shoulder that made me suspicious.

'Your bag as well, Jason.'

'No need, sir. I haven't got a ruler. Mine was nicked last time.'

'No harm checking, Jason. We didn't do it earlier on. And you, Shaun.'

Jason dumped his bag on the floor, opened the zip about halfway and looked inside.

'It's not there.'

'You having trouble with that zip, Jason? Perhaps I can help.'

'Oh no!' exclaimed Jason. 'It's not fair. Someone's trying to put the blame on me.'

'There's not a lot to say, is there?'

Jason and Shaun didn't answer. We'd returned to my office after I'd escorted them to their classroom and concluded my investigations.

'It is possible for someone to put five rulers in your bag without you knowing,' I conceded, looking at Jason, 'but that doesn't explain the hundred and eighty-four rulers in your locker.'

'Who was that girl who said that anything was better than school?' asked Dominic.

'Natalie. Natalie Cromar,' answered Jamie. 'Why?'

'What you said about her was right.'

The shed was a world away from the pool. She'd be back there tonight, but for now she could relax. Ricky was acting like an idiot on the water slide. Paula was trying to get on with Kane and it seemed to be working; she was putting suncream on his back.

'What did I say?' asked Jamie.

'You said she was prepared to put up with anything, and *you* weren't.'

Dominic was smart. He'd started by asking a question. Then, when he gave his opinion it was like a compliment. She couldn't help getting drawn in by it.

'I know what you mean about some teachers being pricks,'

he agreed with her again. 'They don't even like kids. You can tell. They shouldn't be in a school.'

'That's what Proden's like.'

'He should be leaving, not you.'

'Yeah, well, it's not going to happen, is it?'

Jamie had given Dominic a full account of how the teachers were on her back, just looking for an excuse to kick her out. She'd raved on about earning money, being independent and getting away from Pat. Then she'd told him she was leaving school.

'My mother reckoned that unless you've got a good job to go to . . . you should put up with school, because it helps with the rest of your life,' he said.

'So how come you didn't listen to her?'

Dominic paused.

Damn! She'd been too quick. Too blunt.

'I did,' he replied. 'Leaving home and leaving school wasn't part of the plan. I think you're mad if you do it.'

Jamie looked to see if Dominic was serious.

'What do you mean, mad? Which part's so mad?'

'All of it.'

Suddenly, he was a stranger. Why had she said so much? It was like an ambush. He'd let her just talk on.

Breathing tight and shallow, Jamie stared resolutely at the pool, jaw clenched. Her body was stiff with anger.

'D'you want to talk about it some more?' he asked.

'Screw you!' she snapped.

I'd only been awake a few minutes when Gary Hawthorne phoned to say he'd be absent today. He'd been ill over the weekend and was still feeling sick. I began ringing relievers immediately. The first four already had bookings for other schools. I could feel the pressure building. I needed to be in school early.

Apart from organising the allocation of relief lessons and routine matters, there was a long list of other jobs needing my attention, some of which were imprinted on my memory:

'Someone's been lighting fires in the rubbish bins near the gym. It would be worth talking to Warren Horrowitz. One of them contains the smouldering remains of his Maths book.'

'Could you remind the female staff on yard duty to check the girls' toilets regularly? There are numerous girls staying in there and there's a lot of smoke coming out!'

'I'll be sending Nick Kelland to you on Monday morning. I found three new Social Science books with pages stuck together yesterday. Some of the kids told me he was blowing his nose in them.'

Jamie woke when it was still dark, and left before Paula's family opened the curtains. The streets were empty. The lamps threw shadows across the road, and occasionally a car went by with its lights on.

It had occurred to Jamie that it must have been like this for Dominic, every morning on his way to work.

The events at the pool were still churning inside her. Dominic's opinion was something she valued. She hadn't realised how much.

She'd taken his support for granted. Then he'd slammed on the brakes, leaving her stranded.

Nothing would stay still in her mind. Dominic was cool, then he was a pain in the arse. She could put up with Pat, then she had to get out. She was leaving school, then she was going back. What Dominic said was right for both of them, then it was only right for him.

Pat was waiting to have a go at her. That didn't help.

She had to make a decision about school.

Proden was the problem last time. But if she was honest it wasn't just him. She had to concentrate on herself. Jamie cam' had to be switched on all the time. She needed to keep her mouth shut. Press the mute button.

That was a big problem. It hadn't worked yet.

It would be easier to leave.

I noticed Aaron Lee today when I was on duty. He seemed to have some new friends. When I checked why they were heading into the buildings, he told me they were in the Drama Club and showed me a note signed by the teacher.

I said it was great to see them involved so early in high school. I expected front-row seats to all their performances.

After the drill press incident with the diaries, Aaron had been moved away from Warren Horrowitz for most of his classes. Both Warren and Aaron had been spoken to separately, and all teachers had been asked to watch out for instances where Warren might try to get Aaron into trouble.

Aaron's name hadn't cropped up for a while. Perhaps it was working.

'Everything going okay?' I asked Aaron. 'You're managing to stay out of trouble?'

'Yeah.' Aaron nodded. He hung back while the others wandered on. 'I'm going to the speedway tonight.'

'Lucky you!' I looked impressed.

'Stewart's taking us. He's cool.'

The other boys disappeared round the corner.

'Who's Stewart?'

Aaron's sneakers squealed as he turned on the polished tiles.

'Mum's boyfriend.' The answer was tossed back without looking.

He scampered down the corridor.

I hoped Stewart was an improvement on her husband.

I phoned Mrs Reynolds as soon as I could, to see if she'd heard anything from Jamie. I didn't mention that I'd seen her in the Mall.

Mrs Reynolds said Jamie had stayed out all weekend, sneaking back home in the early hours of the morning and locking herself in her room.

'I haven't seen her yet, but she'll get a piece of my mind when I do. I'm not being walked over by the likes of her . . .' It was impossible to get a word in. '. . . She's not using my house as a drop-in centre, coming and going as she pleases. If she wants to be a street kid she can be one – seven days a week, not just at the weekend.'

'I'm glad to know she's safe.'

'What's that?'

'I said, I'm glad to know she's safe.'

'Huh!'

'Well, I've got to go now. It's getting busy here.' I was off the line before she could wind up again.

Doors seemed to be closing all around Jamie. Either she was locking herself in or she was being locked out.

Hanging around school. Nothing else to do.

A lunchtime ciggie with Paula seemed a good idea until they got sprung by some new teacher.

The teacher confiscated Paula's lighter and half-smoked cigarette, and said to follow her inside. Then she glanced back at Jamie. 'I don't think you should be here, Jamie. You're in enough trouble already. You'd better head home.'

What chance have you got when even the new teachers know your name? Jamie had a vision of Wanted posters, with her face on them, all around the staffroom. There was probably one on the staffroom dartboard. She'd always thought Strehborn had left a photo with detailed notes for the new deputy. Perhaps he made up individual information packs for all the new teachers as well.

There was stuff-all to do now. She walked on aimlessly, in the general direction of the shops.

A police car passed her, at reduced speed. She thought it might stop. Every so often the police had a blitz on kids out of school. They reckoned they were usually up to no good. Drugs, shoplifting, graffiti, house break-ins, you name it. They picked them up, questioned them, bundled them into a car and took them back to school.

All the deadheads the teachers hoped would stay away for ever were brought back by special delivery, to start causing trouble again.

Jamie looked at the plain red-brick facades of the houses. The paint on most of the doors and window frames was chipped and faded. Beaten-up old cars slouched in driveways. An unhinged gate sagged on the ground. It had been dragged across the driveway, creating a fan-shaped scar.

Straight lawn edgings were the telltale sign of someone trying to keep a place tidy.

Jamie couldn't remember when she first started noticing these things. Not exactly. But it was after her mother left. Before that, she took everything for granted.

A siren erupted behind the houses to Jamie's left. Police car, no more than two streets away.

Several young kids scrambled out of one of the houses. The sudden growl of a motorbike turned their heads.

Jamie twisted sideways. A dirt bike leapt out of the alleyway alongside her.

'Shi i i i i t!' The rider struggled to avoid her as the bike skidded and tipped over. The back wheel whipped into the loose surface bordering the pavement. Sharp gravel sprayed into her ankles.

'Alex! Ya little arsehole.'

The engine whined, then spluttered into silence.

Alex responded with a stream of abuse. He dragged the bike upright.

'Have ya seen Warren?'

'No!' Jamie scowled vehemently.

Alex jumped on the bike, kick-started it, and flew off over the kerb.

On the far side of the road he jerked the front wheel onto the pavement and roared down another alleyway.

The young kids clung to the wire fence like spiders, staring after him.

Was it only the bike that Alex had nicked, or were there other things shoved in his pockets?

The police would be straight round his house if they knew who they were looking for. It wouldn't be the first time. Cheryl would go mad.

Jamie stopped and tapped some gravel out of her shoe. *Bloody Alex!* It occurred to her that Alex was like an abandoned dog. When Alex was on the streets, he survived on his wits.

He was never in school. But he was never far away either, because that's where the other kids were. It was a way to get some recognition. Pathetic really. He was only around under sufferance. His mother could barely put up with him and her boyfriend prompted him to go into hiding.

She remembered Rob, Cheryl's boyfriend, last time she babysat. Alex had left almost as soon as Rob arrived.

'Did he give you any trouble?' Rob asked pointedly as Alex was leaving.

'No.'

'That's good then, eh?' Rob deliberately raised his voice so that Alex could hear. ''Cause he knows what would have happened if he had.'

He looked at Jamie as if he expected her to agree totally. There was a mean twist to his smile. Did Cheryl ever notice?

I phoned Mrs Reynolds again later in the day, to let her know that Jamie was not allowed on or near the school grounds during her suspension.

There was a snort at the other end of the phone. 'I'll tell her. But it won't do any good. She's been a real moody bitch lately. And she's got a bloody foul mouth on her. I don't know where she gets it from. Is that you, Jamie?'

A door slammed.

'I'm speaking to you, you little cow.'

I pulled the phone away from my ear.

'I'm talking to your teacher, and he says they're not going to have you back. You're a troublemaker. They don't have to put up with you.'

Burst of music.

'Mrs Reynolds, that's not quite right. She can come back if she behaves appropriately. It's all explained in the forms I sent you.'

'What forms?'

No chance to reply. Banging in the background. 'Turn that music down.' Renewed blast. More banging. 'I know you can hear me.'

Footsteps approaching the phone.

I'm adding to the tension. Both sides have got something to prove.

'Mrs Reynolds, I've got to go now, but when Jamie's ready to listen, perhaps you could tell her what I've just said. And I look forward to meeting you on Wednesday morning.'

'She'll be out sooner than she thinks,' said Mrs Reynolds. 'I'm going to make myself a cup of tea, then turn the electricity off at the mains. That'll fix her.'

I made time to call in on the breakfast program this morning. Laughter and chatter competed with the clatter of dishes and cutlery. Somewhere in the background was the sound of a hyped-up DJ on morning radio. The volunteers seemed to relish their work. It was like a little social club.

I complimented everyone on their efforts and joked with Cathy Lee that she must be spending more time at school than Aaron.

She said she enjoyed it. It made her feel useful. She understood what some of the kids were going through. Aaron looked up and waved, while swallowing a mouthful of cereal.

A guy in blue jeans and a black windcheater tapped Cathy's elbow.

'Are these ready to wash up?' He pointed to the cups and plates on a nearby table, then looked at Cathy, anticipating an introduction.

'This is Stewart. He helps out sometimes.'

'Pleased to meet you. I'm Craig Eliot. How often is sometimes?' I asked.

'Not sure,' he laughed. 'I've only just started. It'll depend on shiftwork and overtime.'

'And how did you get involved in all this?' I asked casually. 'Have you got a child at the school?'

'Sort of,' smiled Stewart. 'I help out a bit with young Aaron.'

He stacked the crockery and headed for the sink. He stopped momentarily behind Aaron, balanced everything in his left hand and ruffled Aaron's hair.

Shortly after the start of first lesson Mrs Marlow turned up with Alex and her younger child.

I met them in the foyer and showed them into my office. Mrs Marlow was carrying a plastic bag. The little boy had a firm grip on the side of the bag. Alex lagged behind.

'His dad wouldn't have him. He said it wouldn't work. He was out all the time. So he's still with me.' She paused and looked at Alex. 'But I've told Alex it's his last chance. I've told his dad as well. If Alex doesn't behave, I'm sticking him on the bus and his dad can sort it out. He's got responsibilities as well.'

It's like being tossed into a movie or a play. I'm thrown into the middle of other people's lives for a while, and I'm relieved to know I can step back into my own life again, but that's not true for the other characters. I get glimpses of where they've been in Acts One and Two. I can see where the script is taking them, and wish that I could write them a different ending.

I looked at Alex. He looked away.

'And what have you got to say, Alex? Are you ready to do the right thing?'

No answer.

Alex turned towards his mother. Her face tightened. She glared at him indicating that he should speak. She leaned forward to jab her fingers into his shoulder. He was too quick. He drew away, nearly tipping the chair over. He glared back.

'I warned you!' she snapped.

Alex centred himself on the chair again, with one eye on his mother. 'S'pose'

'And what does "s'pose" mean, Alex?' I asked.

I waited. I could feel the tension in his mother.

'No waggin' school.'

'Anything else?'

'No nickin' things.'

I hadn't been thinking of that.

Mrs Marlow opened the plastic bag. 'He's been going up the shopping centre and stealing things during the day. As soon as I've finished here, I'm taking them back.'

She held the bag towards me. I could see the cap he'd been wearing when I saw him last, along with a sweat top and some sunglasses.

Anger flickered in her eyes as she looked towards Alex. He was grinning. 'You can take that look off your face an' all.' She looked at me again. 'I could hit him at times. I really could. He's a right little shit, 'scuse my French. He's ruining my life.' She turned back to Alex. 'You know what happens if you get in trouble this time. You go back to your dad, no matter what he says. He'll wipe the smile off your face. He'll wipe your head off as well.'

I returned to my previous question.

'So what else, Alex? What else are you going to do to stay out of trouble besides no waggin' and no nickin'?'

Alex looked blank. I gave him a clue.

'I'm thinking of the way that you behaved outside the Maths class the other day.'

Alex grinned. 'No ridin' my bike in the school grounds.'

I waited, 'And?'

Alex glanced at his mum.

'Be polite.'

'Which means?'

'No givin' people the finger.'

'Typical,' exclaimed Mrs Marlow. She raised her hand and leaned forward. Alex slid to the side of his seat. I stretched an arm between them. Mrs Marlow settled back, shaking her head.

'It's got to stop at home an' all. And I'll tell you what else. No more picking on your brother, swearing at me and kicking holes in the wall.' She sank back into her chair. The anger was still there, but now it was desperation I could see in her face.

I called the front office and asked for someone to collect a note from me. I quickly scribbled a message to Angela Davis, asking her to come straight away, if possible. There was a chance that Mrs Marlow would speak to a counsellor if she came now.

The younger child found some Textas on my bookshelf. They clattered loudly onto the floor as he pulled at the packet. He looked around nervously.

I gave him a blank sheet of paper. 'Here you go. You can do some drawings on this if you like.'

His mother shook his arm. 'Behave yourself or you know what'll happen,' she said. 'I'll send you to school.'

It was the second time I'd heard her say that. 'I think

school's a good idea,' I commented.

'It hasn't done Alex any good.'

I smiled and tried to look positive.

'Well, let's hope it will do him some good from now on.'

I gave Alex his timetable and showed him an attendance sheet, which was to be collected from me each morning and returned at the end of the day.

Mrs Marlow took the Texta out of the young child's hand. 'Heath's dad is moving in and we might get married.'

'Sounds like good news,' I said. 'You'll have someone else around to help out.'

I noticed the look on Alex's face. He wasn't impressed.

PISCES

The position of the planets makes this a good time to act. Take control of your love life. Do it now or the opportunity for romance may be lost. If you're not in the middle of a smooth patch in your life, don't worry. It's just around the corner. Money is a problem, so swallow your pride and accept all gifts with good grace.

Turning point — Thursday

Why should Thursday be a turning point? Today should be the turning point. She'd decided to go back to school.

She'd been drifting that way ever since Dominic dumped on her other plans.

He was never far from her thoughts. He was the only person she ever felt eager to be with. It wasn't the all-consuming, pounding-heart feeling that magazine stories described. It was more . . . What would he think? What would he say? What would he do?

She tried to imagine how she'd feel if Dominic came onto her. Maybe there was a switch inside her that she'd turned off, so she couldn't be let down if he wasn't interested.

He was honest with her. He didn't just tell her what she wanted to hear. What happened to her seemed to matter to him. That meant a lot.

Why did she read horoscopes? There were millions of Pisceans around the world. How could one small paragraph be true for all of them? They were crap, but she still thought about them.

Pisceans had multiple personalities and so many moods that they couldn't understand themselves. They were all over the place.

Jamie knew about that; but it was something she wanted to change.

She could take control of her love life by visiting Dominic unannounced. *Throw open the caravan door. Catwalk sensuously towards him, a pocket princess – petite, shapely, smouldering.*

He stares. Riveted, beguiled.

Push the blond dreadlocks back from his face. Lips apart, gaze into his eyes . . .

. . . Then the camera cuts to the wizard's crystal ball, zooms in, and Ricky's sniggering face appears, 'Yeah! Woah! Shit, Jamie. Don't hold back! Dom never said there'd be entertainment tonight.'

She needed to think about it some more. It could go wrong.

Pat was under control. That was a start. Jamie cam' was working for a change. She'd stayed out of arguments by keeping quiet when Pat was going on at her. She didn't even acknowledge that Pat was there.

'I know what you're doing. . . . You're just trying to get me worked up. Well, two can play that game.'

Then Pat would pointedly ignore her, with pronounced rounding of her shoulders, ridiculous sweeping turns and disdainful head movements, trying to be the most silent.

The position of the planets makes this a good time to act.

She'd write a letter to the deputy – get in first before she was asked to fill in a contract or write an apology to Proden. It would show that she'd thought about what had happened.

Whoever thought of the saying, 'Every day is the first day of the rest of your life' had the right idea. You could feel positive about changing your mind all the time.

Jamie could see the funny side of it. She'd had so many first days they'd almost become meaningless. The day she was suspended was 'the first day of the rest of her life' because she was leaving school. Now, today was 'the first day of the rest of her life' because she was going back. And, according to her horoscope, Thursday would be 'the first day of the rest of her life', because it was a turning point.

At least tomorrow should go according to plan.

Dalida Contaris called me over to Home Economics today. There was a problem with Warren Horrowitz.

I was surprised to find that Warren *had* the problem rather than *being* the problem. His diary had gone missing and no one would own up to having taken it.

'Can't trust anyone round here!' exclaimed Warren self-righteously.

'Have you any idea who might have taken it?'

'Nah.'

'It might not have gone missing if Warren had stayed in his place,' Dalida interrupted.

'It's still thievin',' said Warren.

'Okay, everybody. Look up and listen to me.'

The talking quickly subsided. This was better than a lesson.

'I think you all know what's happened. Warren's diary has gone missing.'

Warren stood facing the class, basking in his innocence. It was almost as if he were receiving a prize.

'The first thing I want to do is find the diary. And I won't jump to conclusions about where it's found. . . . If it's found near you, or even in your bag, I understand that anyone could have put it there.'

I glanced at my watch. Plenty of time until the change of lesson. No need to resort to bribery with cans of Coke, yet.

'I'll give you two minutes to check your bags. If you've got cupboards or drawers near you, check them as well.'

Students reached for their bags, then burrowed inside.

Cupboard doors clicked and slammed. Drawers rattled. Hinges squeaked on the oven doors and metal trays jangled as students checked the grills.

'Is this it?'

At the far end of the room a boy with freckles and long hair deposited several teatowels on the side of one of the washing machines, then leaned in again. He pulled out a mangled booklet, with bent covers and torn pages hanging out of it.

'There's some more here.' He re-emerged with damp scrapings of diary pages clinging to his fingers. When he tried to straighten them they came apart, like papier-mâché.

'Fu . . . aar out!' exclaimed Warren.

'I could put it in the dryer, Miss,' the boy volunteered.

Giggling and laughter all round.

'I'll fix it.' A girl at the side of the room was holding up an iron.

'Back to your places, people.' It was difficult to remain serious.

'I'm not getting another one,' Warren protested indignantly. 'Someone's gotta do something about it. I'll make 'em, if I find out who it is.'

'Calm down, Warren. We'll sort something out.'

I pointed at the boy with the diary. 'Can you bring it over here, please.'

He handed it to Warren. Warren peeled it open. It was awash with Texta-colour, leaching through the pages.

The boy squeezed the last drops of water out of the dollop of shredded pages, and handed it to me.

Nobody owned up.

Warren calmed down when I told him his diary would be replaced. He was allowed to leave when the bell rang.

The rest of the class was kept in.

I was keen to avoid a bout of copycat incidents – diaries that were deep-frozen, tumble-dried or toasted.

As the class left, I tapped the shoulder of the boy with freckles and long hair. There was something familiar about him.

'What's your name?'

'Ian.'

'Ian who?'

'Ian Spencer.'

'When did I last speak to you around the school, Ian?'

A friend stopped by his side. I'd seen them both before.

'We were going to Drama Club.'

His mate nodded.

'That's it! I remember now. You were with Aaron.'

They started to move off.

'Ian.' I watched him closely as I spoke. His mate kept going. 'Did Aaron ever tell you about something happening to his diary?'

'No.'

It was less than an Oscar-winning performance, but I decided to let it go.

'Fair enough. . . . It was just a thought, that's all.'

He hurried into the corridor.

I could hear him gathering speed.

I'm getting to know parts of Southside quite well. I haven't been to Danny and Warren Horrowitz's house yet, but I recognised the name of their street from regular reference to their files. Jamie's house was the next street over from Alex Marlow's, on the same block.

I didn't have a lot of time. I had to get back for a meeting. It was best to go during the day. There was more chance of Jamie being home while her friends were in school.

The front door opened before I was halfway up the path.

'You're the deputy, aren't you?'

'Yes. Craig Eliot. How did you know?'

'Recognised you from the photo of new staff in the newspaper. I cut it out and kept it. Didn't think it would be long before I heard from you.'

'And you're Mrs Reynolds?'

'That's right.'

'Pleased to meet you. I've brought some copies of the paperwork we talked about on the phone.'

'You can't trust her. You'll have to send things by registered mail, so I have to sign for it.'

I handed Mrs Reynolds the envelope.

'D'you want to speak to Jamie?' Mrs Reynolds continued. 'Put her straight?'

It was an invitation to speak to Jamie on the doorstep. I wasn't being asked in.

'Yes, if I could,' I nodded. 'I've got a couple of things I'd like to say.'

'You can say all you like,' Mrs Reynolds replied emphatically, 'it doesn't mean to say the little madam's going to listen.'

Mrs Reynolds bustled purposefully into the house. The door half-closed behind her.

'Your teacher's here. You've got to speak to him.'

No response.

'Did you hear what I said?'

Pause.

'Did you hear?'

Door handle rattling.

'It's not me you're dealing with now.'

Banging on the door. It was starting to sound familiar.

'He's a busy man. He's not going to put up with this. You've done it now, you really have.'

Rattle, bang.

'Have it your own way. Stupid little cow!'

Mrs Reynolds huffed irritably as she pulled back the front door. 'She's not coming.'

I held out another envelope, smaller than the first.

'Perhaps you could give this to Jamie.' I said. 'It covers most of what I wanted to say. It would be good if you could slip it under her door.'

Mrs Reynolds turned the envelope over. It was sealed. She would have liked to read it.

'See you tomorrow,' I added.

As I walked to the car, Jamie appeared at the side of the house.

'I came out the back way,' she said, looking over her shoulder. 'I didn't want to speak to you with her around. Sorry about Saturday, in the Mall. I shouldn't have been like that.'

'Thanks. I have to say my wife was less than thrilled about it.' Jamie looked embarrassed. 'I just wanted to confirm that we're expecting you to come and try again tomorrow,' I continued. 'You've got the potential to do well, if you can stay out of trouble for a change. I left a letter for you with Mrs Reynolds, but it only repeats what I've just said.'

There was a curious smile on her face.

'What is it?'

'Nothing really,' she answered. 'A bit of a coincidence, that's all. I was just writing a letter to you.'

'You must be a slow learner,' said Greg Proden.

'Is that right?' I continued searching for the file I needed.

'You've been out visiting again.'

So that was it.

'Do you get a commission for each kid you keep in school?'

'We'll have to talk about it another time,' I said. 'I've got a meeting to go to.'

'Crème de la crème,' Greg mused. 'First that Marlow kid and now Jamie Joel. Surely you've got better things to do?'

'They're just kids, Greg. Sometimes they come good.'

I slipped the file into my bag. 'Excuse me.'

'Jamie's not a kid any more,' he persisted. 'Don't tell me you haven't noticed. Was her mother at home, or did you handle her all by yourself?'

I spun round. 'What are you trying to say?' I demanded.

'Nothing.'

'Rubbish!'

He was avoiding eye contact. He could have been a student I'd picked up for harassment in the yard.

'Just keep your twisted fantasies to yourself. And don't attribute them to me,' I exploded.

'It was a joke,' he mumbled, half-heartedly.

'If something's funny,' I emphasised, 'I'll laugh at it. But that doesn't include tasteless innuendo. Have you got that?' I leaned forward and obliged him to look at me. 'Now I'm late for my meeting.'

I banged the door closed behind me and left him to make his own way out.

A car door slammed outside.

'Mum's back,' said Alex, not moving.

A second door slammed.

'Shit. He's comin' in.'

Alex stamped his heels into his sneakers and shot into the kitchen.

He peered through the doorway.

'Tell 'em you haven't seen me yet.'

Jamie pointed to the soft-drink can by his chair.

'You'd better do something about that.'

Alex swooped on the can, tossed it into a hole in the wall and dashed out of the room.

The front door opened a fraction. A hand grasped the edge, holding it still, to remove the key.

Rob appeared, looking bloated and unsteady. He held onto the door, even when it was fully open.

'Got me own key. Good, eh?' He looked towards Jamie for approval. She kept her eyes on the TV.

'Hurry up, it's cold out here,' complained Cheryl.

Rob let go of the door and half-walked, half-lurched into the room.

He fell sideways onto the sofa, grabbing her shoulder on the way down. His breath reeked.

The grip on her shoulder relaxed. She expected him to let go. He leant against her and raked his hand over her breast.

Jamie flung both arms up and shoved furiously, just as Cheryl came into the room.

'Get off her, Rob. You're drunk.' Cheryl heaved him upright. 'Sorry, love. He's bloody hopeless when he's like this.'

Jamie breathed fast, but she wasn't going yet. She hadn't been paid.

'I'll get him some coffee.' Cheryl went through to the kitchen.

Rob leered at Jamie. She turned away. He was a total sleaze. Anyone could see that.

'Where's Alex?' Rob looked around, then raised his voice. 'Can you hear me, Alex? . . . You'll be a good boy when I move in, won't you? We need to have that little chat Mum promised you.'

'Shuddup, Rob,' hissed Cheryl. 'You'll wake Heath.'

'I haven't seen Alex yet,' volunteered Jamie.

She heard Cheryl checking his room.

'His bike's here.'

'He must have come and gone while I was out the back, playing with Heath.' Jamie was pleased with her own quick-wittedness. 'I was trying to tire Heath out, so he'd sleep better.'

Rob pushed on the seat and stood up.

'Shouldn't drink so much,' said Cheryl.

There was a smirk on his face as he walked out.

'What the hell are you doing with that?' Cheryl asked.

Rob was holding the front wheel of Alex's bike.

'Good one, eh? It'll make sure me and Alex have our little chat.'

Cheryl looked agitated.

'He'll take it out on me.'

'Not if he wants it back, he won't.'

Cheryl picked up her bag, and unzipped an inner pocket.

'We shouldn't be holding Jamie up like this.' She handed Jamie a mixture of notes and coins. 'Check it. I think it's right.'

A loud trumpeting swamped the sound of the TV. Jamie clutched the money and followed Rob and Cheryl outside.

Rob's car alarm began a second, ear-splitting variation. Dogs barked on both sides of the street. Variation number three was under way before he could scramble inside and turn it off.

He glared up and down the street. The alarm had sobered him up more quickly than the coffee. The dogs were still yapping. Rob scoured the street once more, reset the alarm and stomped inside.

'The little bastard!'

Jamie didn't notice anything, but Rob saw it straight away. 'He's got the wheel.' He stormed into Alex's room. 'It was him. The bike's gone,' he exclaimed savagely. 'He must have been round the side, waiting to make a dash for it.'

Jamie laughed to herself. She turned away from Rob, fearful of not being able to hide her amusement.

Alex was living on the edge. He'd won this round, but if Rob got hold of him he'd be dead meat.

Angela Davis informed me that Jamie was left with her aunt for a weekend when her mother went off with a boyfriend. She never came back.

I had another look at Jamie's file before she came in today. Strehborn had put a note in saying, "Old enough to leave school this year. The best solution for all concerned." He'd put a similar note in other files too.

Was he ever challenged to try and turn any of these kids around? I removed the sheets from all the files.

Mrs Reynolds was waiting in the foyer with another woman. I looked at the wording on her T-shirt: 'My next husband will be normal'.

'Hello again. Thanks for coming in.'

Shake of the head. 'Sorry about all this. I can't do anything with her.'

'Hello.' I addressed the woman alongside her. 'I'm Craig Eliot, the deputy.'

'Debbie's a friend of mine,' explained Mrs Reynolds. 'She knows everything that's going on.'

'Is Jamie here?'

'Huh! Little bitch! Wouldn't walk with me. Probably stopped for a smoke on the way.'

I ushered them into the office.

'I don't know what good this'll do,' said Mrs Reynolds, as she sat down. 'She's that stubborn, you can't do anything with her.'

Jamie appeared in the doorway.

'Well, look who's here,' said Mrs Reynolds. 'So glad you could make it.'

'What's she doing here?' Jamie's eyes flared at the sight of Debbie.

'Come in.' I motioned Jamie to sit down.

She sat turning her shoulder on the two women.

I held out a copy of the suspension form. 'We need to start the re-entry process by considering this.'

I explained, in official terms, that Jamie had 'acted in a manner which threatened the good order of the school', and that we needed to talk about what she could do to make sure it didn't happen again.

'What if it does happen again?' queried Mrs Reynolds

'Hopefully it won't. But if it did, we'd be talking about her leaving.'

'Did you hear that?' She pointed accusingly at Jamie.

'What d'you think?' Jamie snapped.

Debbie sighed and raised her eyes. Jamie shot her a fierce look.

'It might be best if you speak to me, Mrs Reynolds, and I speak to Jamie.'

Mrs Reynolds clamped her lips and breathed heavily out of her nose.

I turned to Jamie. 'We need to set some goals for you, Jamie. Have you thought about what you did wrong and some things you can do to make sure you stay out of trouble?'

She seemed to relax. I waited for a reply. Instead, she took a creased note out of her pocket and handed it to me. I had to fold back the corners to open it.

Dear Mr Eliot,

I'm sorry about what happened the other day. I know I was being a smartarse. It wasn't my idea. Someone else thought of it but I was the only one prepared to do it. Things like this always happen to me. It was supposed to be a joke. It didn't mean anything.

I shouldn't have done it and I'll try not to do it again, but I know what I'm like so I won't promise. If you check my records you'll see that I don't usually do the same things again (apart from smoking).

I'm not as bad as I was. Ask Mrs Rowan.

Jamie

'It's nice to get a piece of work with no spelling mistakes in it.'

Jamie gave the hint of a smile.

'But I've read your records,' I tapped a manila folder on my desk, 'and I don't think your letter's quite right when it says that you don't usually do the same things again.' I paused, watching her reaction. 'Why do you think I say that?'

'I can tell ya,' said Mrs Reynolds.

'Get off my back!' Jamie shrieked. 'Why does she have to be here?'

'It's usual for a parent or a guardian to be here,' I said quietly, attempting to calm things down.

'Yeah,' said Jamie, 'so they can stick up for you. But what does she do? She starts putting the knife in like she always does.'

'I have to be here.' Mrs Reynolds chimed in. 'You heard what he said. And Debbie needs to be here because she's moving in.'

'She's *what*?'

Debbie shifted on her seat and looked away.

'You heard! She's got job and rent troubles, so she's moving in with us. Someone has to help her.'

'Moving in?' Jamie looked incredulous.

'Yes, I've given her your room.'

'My room?' Jamie's eyes darted between Debbie and Pat. Suddenly she was on her feet. 'Got it all planned, haven't you? You want everything your own way, so you're getting in reinforcements, two onto one.'

'Jamie.' I raised my voice to gain her attention. It worked, but only until Mrs Reynolds interrupted again.

'Save your breath. She won't listen to anyone when she's in this mood.'

Jamie grabbed her letter from my desk and scrunched it in her fist.

'Just look at that.' Debbie couldn't contain herself.

'Keep out of this,' snarled Jamie.

'Where d'you think you're going?' Mrs Reynolds was struggling to get out of her chair.

'I'm leaving school and I'm leaving home.' Jamie's face was twisted with anger. 'If you could call it a home.'

She marched into the corridor.

'Let her go,' muttered Debbie.

'She'll be back,' Mrs Reynolds called after her. 'No one else'll have her.'

'Dominic will.' Jamie's reply was equally loud.

The name sparked irritation on Mrs Reynolds' face. Clutching her bag, she scuttled to the door and thrust her head into the corridor.

'That's it. Piss off. You can go to hell, you little tart, I wouldn't even let you sleep on the verandah.'

She reeled back into my office, scowling wildly. 'I don't know why I bothered coming. She's not worth it.'

Jamie blazed down the corridor with no idea which way to turn when she reached the door. The people in the foyer were just a blur.

Caught between crying and punching the nearest wall, she shoved the door open and stepped outside.

Turn left. Speak to Paula.

Paula was in Maths. Middle of a double lesson.

The teacher was out of sight. Students nearest the door discreetly let Paula know she was there. Jamie frantically beckoned her out of the room and mimed scribbling a diary note. Anything would do.

A wave of chattering escaped from the room. Paula stepped out, diary in hand. 'What's wrong?'

Jamie's shoulders trembled as she tried not to cry.

'Debbie's moving in, and Pat's given her my room. Fat bitch! Shit, shit, shit.'

'C'mon, don't worry about it.' Paula tightened her hold. 'It won't be for long.'

Jamie pulled away. 'I'm leaving home. I mean it.'

'Where will you go?'

'I'll sleep in your shed, until I can sort something out. I'll . . . '

Paula's expression changed. She pressed her lips together briefly.

'You can't. We're looking after my uncle's dog. His food and everything's in the shed. Dad checks on him, morning and night.'

I'd just tidied Jamie's file away and was about to drink my coffee, when I saw her coming out of the main building. She turned towards the oval, to take the shortcut home.

An exception was justified. She could do the re-entry on her own.

I put the coffee down, moved swiftly into the corridor, through the foyer and cut round the front of the school. Our paths would intersect near the edge of the oval.

I wasn't quick enough. Jamie was ahead of me. I increased my stride.

I could see this becoming ridiculous. I had a fleeting image of myself as a long-distance walker, with swinging arms and exaggerated movements, bearing down on the leader of a race.

'Jamie! Wait a minute.'

She whirled round.

'Can we talk?' I asked.

'There's nothing to talk about.'

'Mrs Reynolds has gone. We can finish the meeting without her.'

She hesitated.

'Sorry, it's too late.' She turned away and started running.

On the way back, I realised that several kids had been watching me. Probably there were faces at the staffroom window as well.

Another cup of cold coffee was waiting for me when I got back to my office. I carried it to the staffroom and tipped it down the sink.

Jamie's shoulders ached. Her bag straps were digging in.

She dumped the bags on the ground and slumped onto a bench outside the supermarket. Morning lessons finished in half an hour. The walk would take Paula about ten minutes.

'You been expelled?' Alex planted his foot on the edge of the bench while remaining seated on his bike.

'Something like that. What are you doing here?'

'Shoppin'.' He reached inside his jacket, pulled out a red sports top, then pushed it out of sight. 'Kids pay good money for 'em.'

Jamie shook her head. 'I'm surprised you're not riding a nicked dirt bike.'

Alex smiled. 'Thanks for coverin' for me the other night. Rob goes psycho sometimes.'

A shiver of revulsion went through Jamie.

'You want to stay well away from him,' Alex added.

'How come?'

'He was talking about you.'

'What did he say?'

Alex floundered.

'What was it?' Jamie persisted. 'Go on, say.'

'It was dirty. Okay?' protested Alex. 'Use your imagination and multiply it by three. He—'

'Oi! You!' A security guard was striding towards them. Alex powered down the mall, standing out of his seat.

The guard broke into a run.

A woman entering the Mall activated the doors from the outside. Alex nearly flattened her as he flew through the gap.

The guard slowed . . . and then gave up.

Rob was vile. She could guess the kind of thing he'd say. He gave her the creeps. Dull eyes, black hair – constant leer. Trouble was, there were plenty more perverts like him on the streets. Despite the bustle of the mall, she felt vulnerable and alone.

A house in Carlton Street had been gutted by fire. It was boarded up, but you could still get in. Kids had levered the wood out of the windows. Jamie had seen needles on the ground outside. She'd probably fall on one when she climbed in. Forget it.

There were social workers who organised emergency accommodation, but they'd try and talk her into going back to Pat's.

There were stacks of half-built houses in the new estate. The security guys never checked them properly. They stayed in their cars. If she broke a window, she could get into one of the locked houses.

Dominic would have her. That's what she'd yelled to Pat. But it wasn't that simple – she didn't want to sleep with him. Boys were thick sometimes. She'd have to spell it out. It would change everything.

She pushed her hand into her pocket in search of a tissue

and discovered the letter from the deputy that she'd taken to the meeting.

Suddenly it meant something different to her. Something more than the message it contained.

A hand on Jamie's shoulder made her jump.

'Sorry I'm late.' Paula linked arms. 'What are you going to do?'

Jamie handed her the crumpled letter. Paula unfolded it curiously. 'What am I looking at?'

Jamie leant over and tapped the neat handwriting at the top of the page.

'You're joking!' exclaimed Paula. 'Are you serious?'

Jamie nodded.

She was pointing to the deputy's home address.

I was right about staff seeing me follow Jamie onto the oval. It wasn't long before there was another version of what happened.

At the end of recess, Greg Proden stopped to congratulate me on my efforts.

'You did well this morning. I hear you got rid of Jamie Joel smartish.' He was almost cheerful. 'The library staff said that after you spoke to her she bolted like a frightened rabbit.'

The events with Jamie should have been enough for one day, but it was just the beginning.

I seem to be spending more and more time following up on kids who are sent to the withdrawal room but don't go. Some of them hide, some wander around the school refusing to respond to the directions of teachers who question what they're doing, and others just go home. Warren Horrowitz does all three – depending on what mood he's in!

The Family Life Team visited the school today to talk to the Year 9s about responsible parenting, sex and contraception. We've had multi-coloured condoms all over the school ever since they left. Condoms on door handles, condoms used in water balloon fights and even condoms on computer mice. I must remember to explain to the cleaners tonight.

The train ride was quick. Ten minutes. Jamie wondered why she hadn't thought of this earlier. It was so obvious.

Mr Eliot knew the situation. He'd seen what Pat was like. He'd be sympathetic.

He wanted to help out. He'd written the letter then taken the trouble to deliver it. He'd followed her halfway across the oval to try and talk to her.

It wouldn't be for long. She could leave her things in his house. She wouldn't have to lug everything around. Only a few days, just until she organised something else.

The bags were hurting.

Not far now. She'd checked a street directory in the newsagent's before she left. She hung around with Paula, almost until the shops closed, to make sure the deputy would be home.

It was nice here. Old and new houses mixed together, with some huge shady trees in the gardens. The deputy would have an old house, with a wide verandah and leadlight windows.

Wrong.

Jamie recognised his car. It was parked under the carport of a new house with black window frames and a black door. You could see a blue and green swing through the wire fencing behind the carport.

It was a bad time to call. He was probably eating or getting the kids ready for bed. Should she wait? No, if she didn't do it now she never would.

Jamie marched onto the porch and knocked decisively on the door.

'I'll get it,' someone called from inside.

It was his wife – she remembered being rude the last time they met.

'Hello. Is Mr Eliot here, please?'

'Hello.' Puzzled look. 'It's for you, Craig.'

'Just coming.'

Jamie strained to hear any whispered conversation. Probably – *What's she doing here? – I don't know. – Well, get rid of her.*

She heard the clatter of cutlery in a drawer.

'Jamie!' The deputy looked behind her, to the top of the drive, for a clue to how she'd arrived. 'What's happened?'

He stepped outside.

'I need somewhere to stay. I left like I said I would. You saw what happened in the meeting. It won't be for long. I won't get in the way. I'll be out all day.'

Stop raving. Get a grip. Jamie cam'. 'I can sleep on the floor. I don't care.' It sounded too much like pleading. Jamie wished she could grab every word back and start again.

The deputy drew a deep breath. He rubbed his chin and covered his mouth with his hand. She'd never seen him searching for words.

'How did you get here?'

What did that matter? He was stalling.

'On the train.'

The baby started crying inside the house. He looked round anxiously.

'I think my wife needs some help. I'd better go and see.'

It was *her*. His wife was the problem. He was worried how she would react. He had to speak to her first.

Before he could move, his wife appeared holding the baby over her shoulder. The toddler was behind, astride a squat plastic car.

'Why don't you come inside and talk?'

'No. It's all right. We're okay here.' The deputy waved her away.

It stung. He didn't want her inside. He wanted his wife to close the door.

'What other options have you considered so far?'

'What?'

'Where else have you considered staying?'

This was making her feel ill. Anger mixed with despair.

'Lots of places.'

'Such as?' He was smiling. More composed.

It was all words. Pushing her away.

'Such as . . .' She couldn't think straight. Her mind was buzzing. She'd banked on staying here.

She grabbed the bag straps and yanked them off the ground.

'Hang on. Let's talk about this.' The deputy moved to take one of the bags.

'Get off!'

Jamie backed away, eyes sparking. 'Aren't you needed inside? You better go in and bolt the door.'

'You've got the wrong idea.'

'Too right I did. I got the idea that you wanted to help. I got the idea that . . .'

The raised voices brought his wife to a window in the front room.

'Don't worry,' yelled Jamie. 'I'm going.'

'Jamie,' he persisted, 'we can organise something'.

Jamie ignored him and shouted towards the window. 'I dunno why you let him out. He's useless!'

Shaun Neale came to see me on his own today. I was surprised to see him without Jason Gillet.

Shaun looked fragile and was soon in tears, as he explained that Jason was picking on him. It was supposed to be a joke, but he'd had enough.

Until recently, Jason just used to call him Shaun, but now he'd started using his surname, Neale. And every time he said, 'Neale', he expected Shaun to literally kneel, or he'd hit him.

Apparently Shaun had spent a lot of time on his knees since I'd seen him last.

Jason was endlessly saying things like 'Hello Shaun . . . Neale', 'Shaun Neale, don't sit', and 'Watch Shaun Neale'.

I told Shaun that I'd have a word with Jason individually. Then I'd speak to them together.

He asked me when I was going to do it.

I said I'd try to do it straightaway, so that he could stay on his feet.

Despite everything else that needed doing this morning, I had to find out what had happened to Jamie.

Nicole and I talked about it on and off all night. It unsettled both of us. Sympathy alternated with exasperation.

'You can't blame yourself.' Nicole assured me. 'She couldn't seriously expect to stay here. Has she got friends?'

'Yes.'

'Well, there you go. She'll be fine.'

She kissed my forehead lightly.

She was right. Jamie was unreasonable. But I still felt I handled it badly.

If anything happened to her I'd feel partly responsible. If I'd reacted differently she might not have stormed off. We could have contacted a crisis care agency and found her somewhere safe for the night.

'Hello, Mrs Reynolds, Craig Eliot here from the High School.'

'If you want Jamie, she's not here.'

'Do you know where she is?'

'No. And if you know, don't tell me.'

'Jamie mentioned someone called Dominic, do you—'

'Don't get me started on him. If she's with him, she'll be pushin' a pram before the end of the year. He's a waster. No job, no brains and no hope. She brought him here once. You should have seen him.'

'Does he have dreadlocks?'

'You know him, do you?'

'Not really. Something I heard, that's all. D'you know where he lives?'

'Somewhere without soap and water. Probably in a cardboard box.'

It was parents' night for the new Year 8s tonight. As usual, many of the parents of students with behaviour problems didn't come. They're about as keen on school as their kids are.

Cathy Lee and Sharleen were serving the chops and sausages. Stewart was there as well. He and Aaron were both wielding long-handled tongs over the barbecue.

Cathy patted Aaron's back then gave Stewart a squeeze. It looked as if the boyfriend thing was getting serious.

Several of the other canteen ladies came with their kids.

Without realising it, they do a lot to promote a positive attitude towards the school. It's good to talk with parents of kids who've settled in happily and are going well.

Peter Meers is not a problem at the minute, but he might be soon, if he listens to his dad.

'D'you do the discipline round here?'

'Some of it.'

'Fights and that sort of thing?'

'I'm sorry, I don't know your name. I'm Craig Eliot.'

'I'm Alan Meers. Peter's dad.' He pointed to a boy I recognised but couldn't have named.

'Pleased to meet you. And how do you think Peter's settling in?'

'All right so far and I want it to stay that way.'

'That makes two of us.' I said with a laugh. 'Do you live nearby?'

He didn't seem to hear the question.

'He's not a big kid, is he?' He nodded towards his son.

'Oh, I don't know.' I wasn't sure what he was getting at.

'That's what I call a big kid.' He was looking at Angelo Ferrini, a boy who stood head and shoulders above most of the other Year 8s. 'If Peter had to fight him, who do you think would win?'

'I hope it doesn't come to that.'

'You're too late. They had a fight in primary school.'

I looked at him inquiringly. He gave me a self-satisfied smile.

'No contest. Peter killed him. It was over in less than a minute. He's been trained, you see. Don't get me wrong. Peter's not violent, but if someone starts something, he'll finish it.'

I was getting the feeling that Peter was some kind of killing machine and we'd all been very lucky that no one had upset him so far.

'What kind of training has Peter had?'

'A mate of mine who used to be in the army taught him the best of several different martial arts. He calls it ACR, it means Attack, Control, Response. If someone hits him once, he attacks them. Then he moves back to Control mode. He controls himself, then looks to see if he's got control of them. It's discipline, see. That's what it is. After an attack you step back for damage assessment. To see if you need to attack again.' Mr Meers was stepping backwards and forwards as he spoke and dissecting the air with his arms, like a Kung Fu instructor. 'Without the Control it would be too dangerous.' He returned to his earlier question. 'So what happens if he hits someone?'

'He could get suspended for two or three days.'

'Is that all?'

I felt as though I'd given the wrong answer in a quiz.

'Well, it depends on exactly what happened and how many times it's happened before.'

'It'll only happen once. He'll hit 'em properly the first time. He won't need to do it again.'

I decided to increase the seriousness of the offence. 'It could be up to five days.'

'It's worth it,' said Mr Meers. 'If anyone gives him any bother, I'll tell him to get stuck into them straight away. Three days, five days, it doesn't matter. Once he's done it, nobody else is going to bother him.'

'It's not a good idea,' I insisted. 'You're best to tell Peter to see a member of staff. If it gets out of hand, the police could be involved.'

'It's still worth it,' said Mr Meers. 'The police won't do anything. Peter's too young.'

I decided to move away. I thought I'd get more sense out of Peter.

The girl was last seen at approximately seven o'clock last night. If anyone thinks they've seen her, or has any information related to her disappearance, they are asked to contact the police . . .

I'd just finished reading to the kids and tucking them into bed. I hurried into the lounge, but the TV announcer had moved on.

I reflected that the last time Jamie disappeared, Mrs Reynolds had shown no interest in notifying the police. Why would it be any different this time? Jamie could disappear without ever being listed as missing.

When do you stop wanting to know that your kids are safe at night?

When they abuse you for checking up on them?

When they lock the door to their room, so it's an instant confrontation if you try to keep an eye on them?

Perhaps the question was irrelevant. Mrs Reynolds wasn't Jamie's mother. She might have always resented looking after her.

I switched channels and was rewarded with another version of the same report.

'Dinner will be ready in a minute, Craig. Have you opened the wine yet?'

'Wait a sec.' A photo of the missing girl appeared on the screen. 'I'm just turning the TV off.'

This was brilliant. Like having your own house. All the doors were open. Thudding music flooded from the lounge into every other room. There was nobody yelling 'Turn the music down', or cutting off the electricity.

Samantha appeared, wrapped in a towel, using a second towel to dry her hair. Straggly lengths of damp, brown hair fell over her eyes.

'What time did we say we'd be there?' she shouted.

Jamie lowered the volume.

'Eight-thirty.'

Samantha wound the towel into a turban and returned to the bathroom. Jamie cranked up the music again.

Samantha's mother was a nurse on night shift. She left home at nine o'clock in the evening, at the latest. Often, like today, she left earlier, to do overtime. When she returned in the morning, she went straight to bed and slept until after midday. It was perfect. The deception was easy.

There was no reason for Mrs Heures to suspect that Jamie was a permanent guest, sleeping in Samantha's room. She assumed Jamie was leaving each night, after she left for work, and Samantha sometimes reinforced that idea, by casually mentioning a time Jamie was expected home.

The greatest likelihood of being found out was if she left things lying around the house.

There wasn't much to remember, really. The mattress had to be slid back under Samantha's bed as soon as she got up. The pillow and quilt just stayed on top. Apart from that, she kept everything out of sight, either in the bottom of the wardrobe or the drawer that Samantha had emptied for her.

'Finished!' Samantha's voice brought Jamie to her feet. 'The hairdryer's still here. I've left it plugged in.'

'Thanks. Just coming.'

Tomorrow night would be different. Samantha's mum was at home. It was her night off. But the problem was already fixed. Samantha had asked if Jamie could sleep over.

Her mum had not only said 'Yes', she also said that she could stay whenever she wanted. Jamie couldn't believe her luck.

This must be the 'smooth patch' in her life that her horoscope said was 'just around the corner'.

Crowds of teenagers swarmed around the wide stairway at the movie theatre. Jamie recognised a few faces, but couldn't see anyone she was looking for.

'Sam. Hey, Sam!' Anton – Samantha's boyfriend. Then the others came into view.

A tremor of excitement swept through Jamie. She'd spotted Dominic. Everyone else was paired off.

Stay calm.

'Where's Ricky?'

'He can't come,' said Dominic. 'Something else on at home. How's everything going?'

'Great. I'm at Samantha's.'

'You've left home for good?'

Jamie nodded emphatically.

'Come on,' urged Samantha. She and Anton were moving towards the stairs. The other couples were close behind.

Dominic took Jamie's hand. She held tight. Her excitement intensified, step by step, as she climbed the stairs.

When they spilled into the foyer it would be like making a public announcement. Everyone would know they were a couple.

I couldn't believe it when I saw Aaron Lee in front of the assembly today. He was one of a group of students performing a short advertisement for a lunchtime presentation by the Drama Club. He even had a few lines to say, which he did with his head up and his shoulders back.

Different kids gave different reasons for going to see the

presentation, such as, 'It'll mean you don't get caught in out-of-bounds areas' and 'You won't get sprung smoking in the toilets'. Then Aaron got a cheer from the audience when he called out, 'You won't get busted hanging around the Library looking up rude things in dictionaries or on the Net.'

Cathy Lee had left the canteen and crept into the back of the assembly to watch. She enjoyed the applause as much as Aaron. As it died down, she gave him a wave and slipped out through the double doors, still beaming.

I made a mental note to congratulate Aaron during the day and to see the performance if I possibly could.

'Have you seen Jamie Joel lately?' I asked Ricky Whan.

'Nah. She's left home, hasn't she?'

I looked at him and smiled. 'So you do know a bit about it then?'

Ricky took it as a compliment. He grinned.

'I want to speak to her,' I said.

'I don't know where she is,' said Ricky. 'I just heard she'd left home, that's all.'

'No one has to dob her in,' I continued. 'I just want her to come in and speak to me and Ms Davis, the counsellor. I don't have to know where she's staying.'

I could see his mind ticking over, trying to work out what was going on.

'Why d'you want to see her?'

'We need to finish a conversation we started the other day.'

'Is she in more trouble?'

I shook my head. 'I thought you might know where she is, Ricky, but even if you don't, I reckon you could find someone who does.'

Ricky adjusted his cap and nodded. This conversation was beginning to make him feel important.

'If I find someone who knows where she is, what do they have to do?'

'They need to give Jamie the message that I want to speak to her, but she'll have to ring first to check that I'm not teaching or doing something else. Can you fix that?'

'I can't promise anything,' said Ricky, 'but I'll see what I can do.'

He wandered off to rejoin his mates. He walked into a barrage of questions. There was some laughing and pushing, then Ricky took off in the direction of the oval with the others all following him.

Looking for work sucked. Jamie had walked in and out of endless shops and fast-food outlets. She always left her name and Samantha's mobile number, but no one called her back.

'You're a bit young', 'We need someone with experience', 'Keep calling in', 'It's a pity you weren't here last week': she'd heard it all.

Despite the Rob factor, she'd even called on Cheryl Marlow, to say she was available for babysitting. That sucked too. Cheryl had booked someone else.

Jamie tried to improve her chances by photocopying Paula's last school report, with her own name pasted over Paula's in several places.

A few people said how good the report was, but it didn't make any difference. She still had no job.

The Social Services office was depressing – queues at the counters, nobody smiling.

On either side of the automatic doors several *Job Search* touch-screen units sprouted from the floor. A middle-aged, bearded guy leaned forward to press a screen. His beer gut moulded itself around the edge of the unit.

Jamie tapped a screen and watched the display dissolve.

A list of job search categories appeared. She pressed *Postcode Search*.

She needed a job close to Samantha's or somewhere she could get to on public transport.

Two jobs: 'Pharmacist' and 'Multimedia Officer'. Each had a button to press for more details. No point.

A girl about her own age vacated a seat in front of one of the *Job Access* computers. Jamie dived into her place, almost like playing musical chairs.

The information link looked promising. Perhaps she was entitled to some money now she was out of home.

She moved the mouse. The cursor stayed where it was. She shook the mouse.

Nothing.

She turned the mouse over.

'Shit!' The ball was missing.

The queues were even longer than when she'd arrived. She'd be waiting for ages.

The woman at the counter spoke loudly, repeating information and broadcasting it to everyone in the line. Jamie was tempted to leave before her turn arrived.

'How can I help you?'

'I've just left school and I—'

'You'll have to speak up, I can't hear you.'

She felt as if a spotlight had picked her out, and she was standing under a *Sad Loser* sign.

I suspended Warren Horrowitz today.

I'd sent a message around all the classes about the dangers

of pellets and elastic bands, and the fact that I'd asked teachers to confiscate them and give any offending student a detention.

I'd also mentioned to one of the teachers that I'd be seeing Danny Horrowitz as soon as I could. He was suspected of bringing bags of elastic bands to school and stringing ten or more together to make catapults which fired paper pellets at twice the speed of sound.

Unfortunately, the teacher mentioned it to Danny before I had a chance to get to him. Danny immediately guessed what I wanted to see him about and gave his extensive arsenal of elastic bands to Warren, in the change of lessons.

Warren, of course, couldn't resist trying them out. He nearly took someone's ear off with a pellet the size of a golf ball. Then he got really upset when the kid who'd been hit, and was in tears, told the teacher it came from Warren's direction.

The rubber bands were subsequently discovered and confiscated.

Warren then found the kid at recess and hit him for dobbing him in. Kids get into fights from time to time, but by all accounts this was pretty vicious.

I spoke to Warren briefly before sending him home. He was in tears, not because of what he'd done, but anticipating what was going to happen to him at home.

'It's not my fault. He dobbed me in. Danny'll go mad.'

'I'll speak to Danny.'

'It won't make any difference'

'You can't just go round hitting people.'

'Why not? I'm gonna get hit because of him.'

The conversation wasn't helping. I decided to save it for the re-entry meeting.

I phoned home and Mrs Horrowitz answered. I told her that there had been an incident during recess, involving Warren.

'What's it this time?'

'Warren hit another student.'

'It was his fault, Mum, honest,' Warren called towards the phone. His voice sounded desperately innocent and on the edge of tears.

'That'll do, thanks,' I said sternly.

'Yeah, well, it don't seem right to me,' his mother responded. 'He sounds really upset. He was probably just sticking up for himself. What's he supposed to do? Just let people walk all over him?'

I explained what had happened.

'Yeah, well, you'd be upset wouldn't you, if someone did something and you lost things which belonged to your brother?'

I briefly outlined the school's policy on violence.

'Just send him home.' She was losing interest in the discussion. 'My boyfriend'll get to the bottom of this tonight. If Warren's really done something wrong, he'll soon sort him out. After a pause, she asked, 'When can he come back?'

I gave Mrs Horrowitz the details of the re-entry meeting, including the necessity for a parent or caregiver to be present.

'It'll be best for me if I don't come,' said Mrs Horrowitz.

'We're trying to do what's best for Warren,' I reminded her.

'It'll be best for him if you don't send him home,' she replied.

'Oh yeah, I nearly forgot. Eliot spoke to me the other day. He wants to see you.'

Ricky was in the doorway of the caravan, trying to stop smoke from his cigarette drifting inside.

'Yeah, good one.'

'Honest. No bull.'

'What about?' Jamie withdrew her arm from Dominic's shoulder and leaned towards the door. Only Ricky's fingers were visible as he hung outside, with his feet anchored to the step.

'Who's Eliot?' asked Dominic.

'The school deputy,' said Paula. 'The one who suspended Jamie.'

'What did he want?'

'Didn't say.' Ricky pivoted back inside. 'Dunno. He said something about finishing the talk you were having before you left.'

'Did you tell him where I was?'

'Course not.'

'He's probably trying to help Pat track me down.'

'Nah. Don't think so.'

Ricky disappeared for another drag on his cigarette.

'He said he didn't need to know where you were staying,' he called out.

'How about telling me everything?'

'That was it. Honest.'

'Ricky!' Jamie raised her voice accusingly.

Ricky swung back inside. 'Oh yeah.' His face brightened as he remembered something else. 'He said you'd have to ring before you went in. To make sure he wasn't teaching. D'you want me to tell him I couldn't find ya?'

'Don't know yet. I need to think about it.'

Dominic slipped his hand around Jamie's waist and pulled her closer.

'If I make the wrong decision, you can tell me I'm mad,' she murmured. 'Like at the pool.'

He tightened his grip. They were both laughing.

The caravan was old and small. Seven people made a real squeeze. A faded plastic shower curtain separated the cramped sleeping section from the living area. It was pushed to one side as Samantha and Anton spilled onto the bed.

'Yeah! Woah!' Kane and Ricky broke into spontaneous cheering. 'Get into it. Don't worry about us.'

Samantha propped herself up to speak. 'Piss off!' She giggled and fell back again.

'How come they get the only bed?' Kane protested.

'It's not the only bed,' grinned Dominic. 'This table lowers to make another one.'

'Well, that's me and Paula fixed up,' announced Kane. 'What are the rest of you gonna to do?'

He puckered his lips and pressed theatrically against Paula, searching for a kiss.

'Get off!'

Ricky started making ape noises in the doorway. A chorus of hooting and stamping broke out as the others joined in.

'Shudup!' Anton's mobile phone was pressed to his ear. 'C. Eliot.'

'What's he doin'?' Ricky had been slow to quieten down.

'It could be C and something else,' said Anton. His face was alive with expectation. 'Is that in Wilton?' He nodded excitedly. 'That's it.'

He quickly thumbed the numbers.

'Hello. Can I speak to Craig, please?'

Stifled laughter. Anton pressed his finger to his lips, pleading for quiet.

'Never mind. Can you give him a message? He wants to see Jamie, but he didn't say how much of her he wants to see.'

Jeers erupted in the caravan.

'Dirty old man!'

'We know what you're after.'

Anton held out his mobile like a boom microphone. The hooting rose to a crescendo.

'Shut up!' demanded Dominic. 'You'll get me thrown out of here.'

Anton put the phone back to his ear. 'She's gone. I'll redial.'

'No!' Jamie was surprised by her own vehemence.

Anton shrugged. He shoved the phone in his pocket.

'What did you do that for?'

'It was just a laugh.' Anton looked around for approval. 'Everyone else thought it was funny.'

'Don't include me,' scowled Dominic.

'Great place for a party, man,' said Ricky, climbing back inside.

'You're going the wrong way, Ricky,' snapped Jamie. 'You need to go outside and look for your brains.'

'Waste of time,' joked Kane.

'Gotta go anyway,' said Ricky. He gave Kane the finger, right up close, in a gesture that threatened to plug his right nostril.

'Shit! And me.' Paula had looked at her watch.

Everyone piled out, the caravan dipping and shuddering each time.

'You coming, Jamie?' called Samantha.

'I'll catch you up.'

She felt Dominic's hand turn her face. They were kissing. Her whole body tensed as his fingers touched her bare skin. She didn't want to have to push him away.

The caravan shook.

They separated instantly.

Tapping on the window.

'What are you two doing in there?' Kane lowered his voice, trying to sound serious. Everything rattled.

'If you don't stop,' Kane's voice wavered, 'the suspension'll break.'

'I'll be there in a sec, ya morons.'

'That's what you said before.'

On a corner shelf by the bed the wizard held out the crystal ball.

'What about tomorrow?' asked Dominic.

Was he asking her back, on her own?

'Come round to Samantha's. About seven-thirty. Her mum won't mind.'

Jamie shivered as she stepped into the night air.

'About time.' Ricky was waiting outside.

'You should still see that deputy, like he asked,' said Dominic. 'Tell him the phone call was nothing to do with you.'

'Huh!' Jamie jerked her head scornfully. 'Fat lot of good that would do now.'

Several lights illuminated the entrance to the Caravan Park. The others were waiting, standing in the shadows.

'Good idea of yours, Ricky,' said Anton. 'I've organised everything.'

'What's that?'

'The party. It's all fixed.'

Samantha smiled diffidently at Jamie. 'It's at our place.'

Jamie glanced silently at Anton. How helpful was that? No wonder he was repeating a year at school. He had a knack for stuffing things up.

'Yes?' Nicole's tone was unusually curt.

'Hello. It's me.'

'Thank goodness.'

'What's wrong?'

'I thought it was another nuisance call. Some idiot kids phoned up about ten minutes ago.'

'What did they say?'

'I'll tell you later.' Her voice was flat.

'Are you okay?'

'I'll be better when you get back.'

The School Council meeting had finished early, but the principal offered everyone coffee and several people still wanted to stop and talk. I hurried home as soon as I could.

'What's the idea of giving school kids our number?'

The question had obviously been simmering for some time.

'Hang on. Let me get inside. I didn't give the number out. We're in the book. They can find it on their own.'

Nicole stared at me. She ran a hand through her hair. The house was silent. The table lamps in the lounge cast broad shadows across the room.

'First, you gave them our address and now they've got the phone number. Is this what we can expect from now on – kids throwing tantrums on the doorstep; obscene calls late at night? Perhaps they'll come round and throw rocks on the roof. How do you think Marc and Renae will react to that?'

'What do you mean, obscene phone calls?'

Nicole glared at me. 'It was that Jamie girl again.'

'What did she say?'

'Nothing. It was a boy's voice, but he was talking about Jamie. He said you wanted to see her. Then he made some coarse remark about how much you wanted to see.'

Tension lodged in my throat, like a bitter taste. Ricky. I shouldn't have spoken to him.

'This isn't part of the job, Craig. It's all gone wrong.' She shuddered.

'Was it just one voice?'

Nicole shook her head. 'There were others in the background, laughing and calling out suggestive comments.'

There was a pause as I contemplated what she'd said.

'I want a silent number,' Nicole insisted. 'It's not just me. You know Marc picks up the phone.'

'I'll get onto it first thing tomorrow.'

There was no reply.

'I'm sorry, Nic.' I wrapped my arms around her and hugged her tight.

She kept her arms at her sides. She was stiff, tense. I could feel my anger growing. This was right over the top: intruding on home life, alarming Nicole. Besides which, it could blow out, start rumours. And people don't check rumours before passing them on. They develop a life of their own.

Paula Fiorito was waiting for me in the foyer. Apart from seeing her in the Mall with Jamie and giving her a first warning for smoking, I didn't know much about her.

She came to tell me that Jamie would be in at eight-forty tomorrow, if that was okay.

I tried to disguise my surprise.

'Is that a problem?'

A part of me wanted to yell, 'Yes!' What the hell did she expect after that phone call?

'No, no. Of course not. But ask her to make it about five past nine. Everything's more settled by then. And thanks for bringing the message.'

As soon as she'd gone, I checked Ricky Whan's timetable. He had Tech. Studies with Gary Hawthorne. I didn't need to ask to speak to him. He was outside the workshop, leaning against the wall. He straightened up when he heard my footsteps.

'I knew I was right, talking to you the other day.'

For a second he looked confused.

'I haven't seen Jamie yet, but I think she's coming in tomorrow,' I continued. 'I reckon it's you I've got to thank for that.'

Ricky relaxed.

'Yeah, right. Paula Fiorito came to see you, did she? I thought she would,' he said. 'I told her there was nothing to worry about.'

'Thanks,' I replied, looking him in the eyes. 'Whatever you said, it did the trick.'

I decided not to mention the phone call, but I needed to remind him I wasn't completely blind.

'I'm not sure why you're out here, Ricky, and I don't want to know at the minute. But I may have to speak to you about it later on.'

Ricky grinned.

'Mr Hawthorne'll be all right,' he said. 'He just takes a while to calm down.'

Aaron Lee's emergency card was left on my desk to initial before re-filing. There had been a change of address. He and his mother were now living with Stewart, and Stewart was listed as the emergency contact person, to be called if Cathy was unavailable.

When Cathy spotted me on yard duty, later in the day, she immediately left the canteen and scurried towards me.

'You'll never guess what's happened. It's fantastic for me and Aaron.'

'Tell me,' I smiled.

She handed me a folded newspaper.

'Read that article down the bottom.'

'"Man Hits Policemen"?'

'That's the one.'

It was about a drunken motorist who assaulted two policemen when he was pulled over for breath-testing.

She didn't wait for me to finish reading.

'That's my ex-husband, that is. And it's not his first

offence.' She was grinning from ear to ear. 'With any luck, he'll get at least three years.'

I called by to see Alex Marlow's mum on the way home from school today. Alex had been absent for the last three days. He only attended for a day and a half. She said he'd gone off his head because her boyfriend was moving in.

She pointed to an inside door which had black scuff marks and a jagged hole right through the bottom of it.

'That's what he did. Well, he's gone now, so I can start getting my life back together.'

'Where's he gone?'

'I put him on a bus and sent him to his dad's.'

'Was his dad okay about that?'

'I didn't give him a choice,' she said angrily. 'I put Alex on the bus before I phoned to tell him about it.'

I waited to see if she was going to say more.

'He wasn't happy. But that's too bad. I just put the phone down on him.'

Several times today I've thought of Alex sitting on that bus. What do you think about when you're being sent from one parent who doesn't want you, to the other parent who wishes you weren't coming?

I told Nicole about it. I needed to speak to someone. She was astounded.

I have a sense of wanting to cry inside. And I'm not sure who to cry for, the child or the parents.

Jamie placed the last two boxes of chocolates on the pile and repositioned the price card on top.

A stroke of luck. Someone had quit an hour before she walked into the cheap goods store. The manager was under pressure. She scored well on some quick-fire mental calculations, so he rostered her for the checkout, after lunch, when he had time to keep an eye on her.

She couldn't wait to tell Dominic.

The only problem was tomorrow morning's meeting with the deputy. She couldn't mention school to the manager. He'd put her off.

She'd tell him she had a doctor's appointment. If he got funny about it, she wouldn't go. She needed the money. School could wait.

Jamie Joel came in this morning. I asked Angela Davis to be there.

She looked small, almost fragile, sitting in the foyer – very different from the angry teenager at my front door.

She told us she was staying with friends. She said Mrs Reynolds didn't give a stuff. There was no way she'd go back.

'This might be a good time to clarify something,' I suggested. 'You've just said that Mrs Reynolds doesn't give a stuff, but, if I remember correctly, the last time we met you had similar concerns about me.'

Jamie fidgeted apprehensively.

'I think your exact words to my wife were, "I dunno why you let him out. He's useless".'

I was conscious of a wry smile on my face.

'Using your words,' I continued, 'do you think I give a stuff, or do we still have a problem?'

Jamie lowered her head. Her face reddened. She slowly shook her head. 'I wouldn't be here if there was.'

She looked directly at me when she spoke. I took it as an apology.

She said she wanted to come back to school, but was thinking of having a break and making a fresh start next term.

I tried not to push too hard, but encouraged her to start straight away. The longer kids are out of school, the harder it is to return. I told her that this could be the re-entry meeting, without Mrs Reynolds. We agreed to talk as if she was coming back within the next few days. If it didn't happen, everything we decided could apply later on.

In the quiet of my office, Jamie was calm and articulate. She knew all the right answers. She knew she did things to impress the other kids. She knew she had a quick temper. She knew her language was inappropriate at times. But she was less clear when I asked how she was going to ensure the unacceptable behaviour would stop.

'You've given assurances and not kept them before, Jamie. So what's going to be different this time?'

Silence. She was thinking about it. I let the silence run, to avoid putting words in her mouth.

'Sometimes I imagine I'm being filmed – I'm outside, watching myself.'

'Does that help?'

'If I imagine it soon enough.'

'Well, that's a start. And what else could be different?'

'I'll try and think before I say things. But I can't promise. I know what I'm like. I just lose it sometimes. I go right off.' She was quickly talking herself into not caring.

'Are you concerned about what you've done when you calm down?' Angela asked.

'Yeah, but it's too late then.'

'Would it help if we changed any of your classes, to move you away from other students?'

Slight shake of the head.

'Perhaps we can do some things which will help make a difference,' I said

Jamie looked up. Her expression didn't change.

'You'll be on a lesson-by-lesson report card for a while, to help you remember to do the right thing all day.'

'I'd better stay on it for the rest of the year.'

'You could be right,' I laughed. 'But the aim is to get you behaving properly without needing a card. We don't want you becoming dependent on it. Not report cards and cigarettes!'

She smiled ruefully.

I paused to try and get the words right. 'I'll be honest with you Jamie. I'm really worried about the first few weeks. I don't often gamble, but if you asked me to put some money on what's going to happen, I reckon I'd be betting that you lose it and go right off a couple of times. And what do we do then?'

'I'll have to leave.'

'We'd all be trapped,' I said. 'And in some ways I'd be more trapped than you. I wouldn't have any options left. The teachers, the parents, even some of the kids would be up in arms if I tried to treat you differently. They would, wouldn't they?'

Jamie nodded.

It felt strange as I listened to the Deputy Principal in myself speaking. The parent in me wanted to offer something less final, as you would for your own children, whatever strife they got into. But schools can't offer that or they start to fall apart.

'There's one more thing that Ms Davis and I have talked about,' I continued, 'but it relies on you to get it right. We'll inform all your teachers that you have permission to leave the class at any time, if you think you're going to lose it. It's a sort of safety valve, to let you calm down before you do something you regret.'

'Where do I go?'

'There are a couple of possibilities. If you manage to calm down outside the room, you could go back in. But it might be a mistake. Why do you think I say that?'

'I might still be mad.'

I nodded. 'You can't afford to get it wrong. It's probably best to stay out until the end of the lesson, then go to your next class, or go to the office and ask to speak to a staff member. You may have to wait, but you can go to the library and get on with some work while you're waiting. How does that sound?'

'Sounds okay.'

'Good. But there are a few conditions to talk about as well.'

She stared at me.

'This system is only for emergencies. I don't want you going in and out of classes like a yo-yo. I also want to know where you are if you walk out of a class. That means you'll have to be outside the room, at the front office, in the library, or with a specific member of staff. If, for instance, you decided to use the system to nick off to the toilets for a quick smoke, that's when the support stops.'

I paused to let the words sink in.

'Is there a particular teacher you'd like to go to, if you need to talk things through or ask for advice? You don't have to say now. You can think about it.'

'Mrs Rowan.'

'That was quick.'

'She's not out to get me.'

'I'll ask her. I'm sure it'll be okay. If you get this right, you'll help us all out,' I continued. 'I won't have to make decisions that I don't like making. You'll be in control of

what happens to you in school. And Ms Davis will be able
to get back to the other kids who need her help.'

Jamie said she'd phone, as soon as possible, to let us know
what she'd decided.

There was one question I wanted to ask before she left.

'You don't have to tell me, but who's Dominic?' I asked.

'My boyfriend. He lives in a caravan.'

I was tidying my desk when Jamie reappeared. Angela had
just left.

'Did your wife say anything about a phone call?'

'Yes. She not only said something, she was quite upset by it.'

'It wasn't me. It wasn't my idea,' Jamie insisted.

'I'm glad to hear it.'

'I told him it was stupid.'

'Who's him?'

'I can't say.'

I looked at her inquiringly.

'I can't. You know I can't.' She turned away, paused and
looked back. 'I wanted you to know it wasn't me, that's all.
And it wasn't Dominic.'

She was gone before I could reply.

'Relax. No one'll go crazy.' Anton tried to put Samantha's
mind at rest.

Everybody had been given strict instructions on when to
arrive. Samantha told them several times. Nine-thirty: thirty
minutes after her mother's latest possible departure. They
couldn't rely on her leaving early to do overtime.

As it was, she left at eight. So Samantha phoned Anton and
asked him to come early.

He arrived with the jumbo snackpacks they'd bought during the day. People were bringing their own drink. If they got hungry they'd order pizza.

'I'm moving anything that can get knocked over,' Samantha announced. 'Jamie, can you organise the glasses? Anton, put a bucket and some cleaning gear in the laundry. And bags for the rubbish, so we can get rid of it all.'

Jamie hadn't seen Samantha like this before. She could see her becoming a nurse like her mother – perhaps even a matron.

'Stop stressin', Sam. It'll be all right.' Anton persevered.

'What about Brad Parker's eighteenth?' Samantha demanded. 'So many glasses got smashed you needed to be an Indian fakir to go in the kitchen. And after his brother puked on the wall, they stripped the wallpaper trying to get it off.'

'That was different. We haven't got maniacs coming. If anyone gatecrashes we'll piss 'em off.'

'The second anyone starts looking sick, give them a bucket or drag them into the garden,' said Samantha.

'No worries. I'll stick Ricky's head in a bucket as soon as he gets here.'

'I thought you said you couldn't get any money.' Dominic looked puzzled.

Jamie was on his lap, legs spilling over the arm of the chair. They were enveloped in pounding music, dim light and the buzz of picture frames vibrating on the wall.

'I got it wrong. The counsellor checked. It's different for me because I haven't got parents.'

Between kisses, she was explaining everything.

The explanations decreased. The kisses grew longer, unexpectedly intense. Suddenly his arm brushed across her breast.

Jamie cam'. The picture flickered, as she eased back, arms braced against his chest.

She saw the spark of irritation in his eyes.

'So, it's Tuesday you go back,' he said, avoiding her gaze.

'Mmm. I'll have a day to get organised. Quit the shop and that kind of thing.'

'Will you stay here?'

'Sam said her mum might let me move in properly, now she knows me better. No hiding. If Pat rings it won't make any difference.' A wriggle of excitement. 'I can't believe how everything's working out.'

Boisterous yelling in the kitchen. 'Good one, Ricky!'

'Don't worry, Sam,' called Anton. 'We got most of it in the sink.'

Samantha groaned in the middle of changing CDs.

Anton appeared, escorting Ricky to the toilet. A plastic shopping bag was hooked over his ears. Shadowy fluid rolled from corner to corner in the bag.

Apart from Ricky, it was going well. No one was stroppy or riotous and after some hassling, the smokers were staying outside.

The clean-up would be a bummer though. There were people everywhere.

'This is for you.'

Dominic held out a small package, neatly wrapped in recycled paper, with a yellow bow.

'It's not made of pewter, is it?'

He laughed and shook his head.

Jamie kissed him spontaneously.

'You don't know what it is yet.'

'I don't care.'

She painstakingly undid the bow. She was going to keep it. The wrapping paper as well.

She gasped as the wrapping came apart. A mobile phone!

'Are you sure?'

'It's not top of the range,' said Dominic.

'It's fantastic.'

Dominic saw the slight hesitation when she looked at him.

'I've been doing overtime,' he explained. 'It's prepaid. When the money's used up, you'll have to pay for the next lot yourself.'

'Same as Samantha's,' Jamie replied. 'It's brilliant. I'll make it last. I won't use it all the time.'

'That'll make two of us.' Dominic put his hand into his jacket and pulled out an identical phone.

Her arms wrapped around him again. She nestled close.

'I charged the battery last night. Check it,' he whispered.

Jamie pressed the On button. A welcome note flashed onto the screen.

Always by
your side.
xxx
Dominic

An outcry in the front garden stifled any response. Angry voices, getting louder.

'What is it?' What's going on?'

A returning smoker pointed to the front door.

'Some old woman, bitchin' outside. Must be a crabby neighbour. It's bullshit. No one's breaking bottles or doing burnouts.'

Jamie raced to the window. Her heart plummeted.

It was Samantha's mother.

The party was wrecked. Kids clustered at different points along the road, in driveways, on corners, around cars.

Mrs Heures was seething, blasting the last kids to leave.

While Samantha vainly tried to calm her mother down, Jamie grabbed her belongings and slipped out of the house.

She could still hear Mrs Heures ranting from over the road. 'I wasn't feeling well and now I feel a whole lot worse. Too right it won't be happening again.' *Slam*.

Jamie felt the shudder. Her door to refuge had closed.

'What are you going to do?' asked Dominic.

She looked up and down the street, as if inspiration might come from something she saw. A surge of emotion swept though her – the caravan. It was in both their thoughts.

She avoided looking at him.

'Cheryl Marlow,' she said, thinking aloud. 'I could stay with Cheryl Marlow.' It would do for now.

'How far away is it?'

'About twenty, thirty minutes. Round the back of Pat's.'

Dominic picked up the larger of her two bags and slung it over his shoulder.

'D'you want to ring first? Use your mobile?'

'She's not on the phone.'

No sign of Rob's car. Good.

The Marlows' doorway was partly illuminated by a nearby streetlight. Enough to see the stem of a broken globe in the outside light socket.

The TV was blaring. Jamie knocked hard.

A head peeped round the side of the door. Alex.

'What are you doing here? I heard you'd been sent to your dad's.'

'He brought me back. What'd you want?'

'Where's Cheryl?'

Alex was fully visible now. He raised his hand to acknowledge Dominic. 'At work.'

'Who's babysitting Heath?'

'Me. She won't leave him with Rob any more 'cause he stuck him in the car and took him to the pub.'

Jamie hovered over her bags, biting her lip.

'Will your mum be back at the usual time?'

'Should be.'

'Okay if I come in and wait for her?

'Up to you.'

Jamie turned to Dominic and squeezed his arm. Alex stared silently.

'I'll be all right now,' Jamie insisted. She rested her arm on Dominic's shoulder and kissed him lightly. 'Thanks for walking me here. I'll ring you tomorrow and let you know what's going on.'

Noise at the door. Dominic, coming back for something?

Key turning.

Wrong. Must be Cheryl.

Wrong.

A shoulder. A T-shirt.

Jamie lifted in her seat. Her stomach muscles tightened.

After several attempts, Rob pushed the key into his jeans pocket. His right arm hung at his side, dangling a six-pack.

When he saw Jamie, the curl of his lip moulded to a grin.

'Can't take me kid for beer, so I'm bringing it home. Good one, eh?'

He dropped the beer at Jamie's feet and tore at the packaging. He fumbled for an opener on his keyring. Froth dripped into her lap as he leant over her with an open bottle.

'You're not going to ask for a glass, like some posh tart, are you?'

Jamie pushed the bottle away and scrambled over the arm of the chair.

'Bitch!'

Jamie grabbed both her bags and dragged them with one hand, reaching with the other for the front door.

Too late. Rob lurched past her and fell against it. The bottle in his hand, cracked solidly against the wood.

'Forgot your drink,' he taunted, deliberately splattering beer over her head.

The weight of his arms pushing down was too much. She sank into the corner, trapped between doorjamb and wall.

A dull metallic thud suddenly echoed round the room. Rob buckled away, cursing with pain. His beer bottle shattered as it hit the tiles.

Alex was hopping up and down as if his feet were on fire. Both hands were wrapped round the handle of an electric frying pan. With a swing like a two-handed tennis player, he pounded it into Rob's knees.

Rob toppled back, unable to avoid landing on broken glass.

Alex looked frantically at Jamie. 'Get out!'

He wound up again, then hurled the pan at Rob. The metal cracked into Rob's wrists, in front of his face. Rob recoiled, jerking with pain, shaking then cradling his arms.

Alex bolted out of the room.

Jamie jumped to her feet and picked up her bags. Glass jagged into the door and scraped across the floor as she pulled it open.

Rob seemed crumpled and dazed. He didn't look up. He was staring at the blood seeping from cuts on both hands.

'Dominic! Dominic!' Jamie hammered the side of the caravan.

'What happened?' Dominic's eyes were wide with concern.

'Rob turned up. Two seconds after you left.'

She still felt shocked. The whole scene was replaying in her mind.

'Can I stay here?' she blurted out, dumping her bags on the floor. She was startled by her own directness.

'Sure. No problem.'

There was more she had to say. 'I didn't want it to get to this. It's been so good. I don't want things to change. I want it to stay cool between us.'

This was impossible. It left out the main thing she wanted to say.

'If I stay here, I'm not sleeping with you!' Jamie exclaimed. 'There, said it. Okay? So if you're going to get shitty, I'll leave now.'

She saw the discomfort on Dominic's face.

The thought of struggling into the night with her bags for a third time was too much.

She began to cry.

Warren Horrowitz returned to school this morning. His mum came with him for the re-entry meeting. He was much calmer than when he was suspended, but his ideas about what he'd do differently next time were a bit of a worry.

'I won't hit kids for Danny. He can do it himself if he wants to.'

'We don't want anyone hitting anyone, Warren. Danny included.'

Mrs Horrowitz said that her boyfriend had told both the boys not to go hitting kids at school. If they had something to sort out, they should do it out of school.

I asked Warren if he realised that what he had done was wrong.

'Say yes, Warren,' his mother responded quickly. 'I want to get home.'

It was impossible to see Warren staying out of trouble, given his mother's attitude.

We established some behavioural goals for Warren and I told him that he would be included in an anger management group that was being run for some junior school boys who needed to develop greater self-control. Then I pointed out what would happen if he was suspended more than three times.

'Fair enough. You heard that, didn't you?' Mrs Horrowitz asked Warren. 'If you keep doing this, you'll be going back to that place they sent you to in primary school.'

'I won't go,' said Warren.

'He's not joking,' said Mrs Horrowitz. 'He didn't go much when they sent him last time. I only found out when he came home in a police car because he'd been housebreaking.'

We heard from Jamie during the day. She was supposed to start school yesterday, but didn't turn up.

Angela had phoned Mrs Reynolds to see if she knew where Jamie was. She said she didn't care as long as she stayed there. Angela noticed that she didn't use Jamie's name once. She used terms like 'bitch', 'cow', 'slut' and 'tart' instead.

Jamie's message was light on details but it was equally worrying. Something had gone wrong with the people she was staying with. She'd moved out. She still wanted to come to school but it wouldn't be for a while. She was staying with Dominic at the Caravan Park.

The job's still eating into family life, but I think it's getting better. It should settle down more as I get used to it. I hope so.

When Nicole gets annoyed, it's as much for my sake as anything else. I'll only get one chance to see my own kids grow up. I felt quite guilty when she pointed out that I've taken far fewer photos of Renae than I did of Marc after he was born.

It's a question of getting the balance right – keeping things in perspective, not getting too involved.

Jamie stared at the wizard. Slivers of light emanated from the crystal ball, creating a web pattern on the wall. It was ironic. She'd only ever pictured Dominic here, looking at the wizard, wondering what lay ahead.

Better than being with Pat – all that moaning and complaining. Perhaps getting lumbered with your sister's kid made you like that.

The drab interior of the caravan had already changed. There was a clip-on lamp fixed to a shelf above the table and she'd put some posters on the walls. Working in a cheap goods store had its benefits.

They weren't really arguing, but lack of space produced tension. Like Dominic adapting to the lowered table still being her bed when he left early for work. He burnt his hand on the stove once, trying to manage in half-light. She heard him swearing under his breath.

If Dominic objected to something, she tried to back off. It was his caravan.

The relationship was more self-conscious; less relaxed.

The news of them being together was everywhere by now. Everyone presumed they were screwing like rabbits.

They'd agreed on a two-week trial. She wasn't sure what she'd do if it didn't work out.

It was the swimming carnival today. The pool was a twenty-minute train ride away, with a ten-minute walk at either end. Most of the staff went with the kids on the train. I was one of the people scheduled to take a car for emergencies and for ferrying any troublemakers back to school, or home, if necessary.

The carnival started late because the train was delayed. Nick Kelland decided to hang on the emergency lever. Staff said he didn't know what he'd done to start with. He said he thought it was something to hold on to when you were standing up. Apparently he can't read.

We tried to contact Nick's parents by phone, but no one was home. He was separated from the other students during the day, to suppress some of his instant hero status.

Staff gave me the names of several other kids who were on the train but not at the carnival. They all said their parents had given them permission not to go. They were going to the shops and games arcades in the city instead.

Cathy Lee was there, supporting Aaron as usual. He was in all the novelty events. She was taking photos, jumping up and down so much the pictures will all be blurry.

An hour after the start, Greg Proden told me that Warren Horrowitz was hanging around the turnstiles, calling out to other students. He was refusing to come in.

I wandered over.

'Hello, Warren.'

'I'm just going.'

'It's a bit early to be going, isn't it?'

'Nah, because I'm not here.'

'Hang on a sec,' I faked rubbing my eyes. 'Yeah, it still

looks like you. You had me worried for a minute. I thought I might be seeing things.'

Warren grinned. 'Yeah, but I'm not here for the swimming. I just came to see some of me mates.' He was genuinely oblivious to any problems with what he was saying.

'Warren,' I put an edge on my voice. He stopped moving. 'I want you to come in here while I phone your mum.' I was about to add 'and we can sort things out', but he took off again.

'Gotta go.' He broke into a run.

I rang home.

'Is that Mrs Horrowitz?'

'Who is it?'

'It's Craig Eliot here, the Deputy Principal from the High School.'

'Yeah, what d'you want.'

'I'm phoning about Warren. Apparently he's not at school today.'

'Yeah, that's right. He's ill, so I said he could stay home.'

'How ill is he? Because I've just seen him here at the swimming pool.'

Slight hesitation.

'He had to fetch some shopping for me.'

'He looks as though he might be a lot better now.'

'No he's definitely ill. But it doesn't mean he has to stay at home all day, does it? As a matter of fact, I'm ill myself today. That's why I had to send him out shopping.'

'Well, if Warren's ill, I suggest he stays right away from school or any special events, like the swimming carnival.'

'It's okay for you to say that. But how am I supposed to keep him at home if he wants to go out? I can't tie him up, can I? And my boyfriend's not here to do anything about it.'

'Perhaps you could tell him that if he's well enough to go out, he's well enough to go to school.'

Another pause.

'Yeah, okay. But he was real sick today, so I'll do that next time.'

Angela and I went back to school via the Caravan Park, to see if we could find Jamie.

Angela had informed a youth support service of the situation, but it was unclear how quickly they'd be able to follow things up. She'd brought some information pamphlets and contact numbers for emergencies. She wanted to remind Jamie she could contact her any time to talk about anything from accommodation to contraception.

We asked around and found the caravan. It was pretty run down, with grass growing over the wheels. There was nobody there. Angela scribbled a note to leave with the pamphlets. I noticed that she'd included her home phone number and reminded her of the problems it could cause.

We left mobile numbers instead.

'Well, look who's here. Hi, Alex!' Angela waved to Alex Marlow. I waved too.

He was leaning over his handlebars, peering round a caravan, several sites away. A livid bruise highlighted his cheekbone. The eye was swollen, partly closed.

He quickly retreated behind the caravan and was gone.

'What a mess,' sighed Angela.

'His eye or his whole life?' I asked.

'Both.'

Jamie slipped the pamphlets back into the plastic pocket. The deputy kept trying. You had to say that much for him.

She rummaged in her bag and took out her phone. She couldn't see herself contacting the counsellor or the deputy on their mobiles, but it didn't do any harm to store the numbers. In a strange way it made her feel less alone.

The open door rattled and the van lurched sideways.

'Hello, Jamie.'

Her body seized. It was Rob, closing the door behind him. She tried to breathe deeply, fending off a wave of panic.

'I was right, eh? Thought it was you.'

She put the phone down, hands at her sides. She wanted to push off the seat and run, but he was blocking the door. The van suddenly seemed ridiculously small and cramped.

Look unconcerned. Do something, anything to look relaxed.

She pulled a tissue out of her pocket and blew her nose.

'Hi, Rob. Didn't expect to see you here. I thought you were Dominic. He's due back any minute.' As soon as the words left her mouth, she could hear how thin and unconvincing they sounded.

'Unexpected pleasure, eh?' Rob leaned across the table.

He slid closer. The smell of beer made her feel sick.

She moved towards the sink. Rob shifted towards the door. It was like a bizarre dance.

She opened a cupboard a bit too hastily, conscious of the chill going through her and the need to hide it. *Be calm; cool, not shivery.* He wasn't just a moron. He knew what he was doing, every time.

'I'm looking for a dry biscuit. I've been feeling sick all day.' She remembered a guest speaker in primary school telling them to be repulsive if they were in danger. Fine. She was just about ready to dribble and puke.

'How come you ran off the other night? Looking for Dominic, were you?' Rob sneered. Jamie could visualise the ugly line of his mouth.

'Yes.' She couldn't think of anything else to say.

She sat down again, at the end of the table this time, opposite the door. *Best to wait. Don't force a confrontation. Play for time.* 'He went to Ricky's. He'll be on his way back now.'

'I don't think Dominic's coming. Do you?'

Involuntary reactions let her down. She knew Rob had seen the frightened flicker of her eyes.

He grabbed her wrist. His hold slipped then tightened. His skin was clammy.

With her other hand she felt for the phone. 'What are you on about?' She trailed her fingertips over the keypad, and pressed the Send button. 'Let go my arm, now. You deaf or something?' *Keep talking. Sound as if you're in control. Cover the noise of anyone answering the phone.* 'You can't just barge into Dominic's caravan—Hey, that hurts! Let *go!*'

'Who's going to stop me?' He was enjoying himself.

Had anyone answered? Were they listening? Perhaps it went to voicemail. Perhaps it rang out . . . Please, no.

'Come 'ere.' Rob pulled her towards him. His breath wafted into her lungs. His face was sickeningly close.

I left school early tonight. The swimming carnival generated fewer incidents than a normal day. After returning from the caravan park, I went through the mail, then phoned Nicole let her know that I was on my way home.

The phone rang as I was putting my bag in the boot of the car.

'Hello. Crai–' I stopped. Somebody was in full flight, already talking . . . 'That hurts! Let *go!*' A girl's voice.

There was something familiar about it.

'Who's going to stop me?' A man. 'Come 'ere.'

'Let go or I'll scream.'

'Scream, and I'll belt ya.'

It was like listening to a radio play. The nagging recognition of the girl's voice was still there, but I couldn't put a face to it.

Grunts, rattling sounds.

'Dominic'll be here soon. He . . .'

I dived into the car. My stomach churned as I backed out of the carpark.

I crept a red light and fixed the seatbelt as the car gathered speed.

'What've you got?' The man's voice was enraged. 'Hey! Give us your fuckin' phone. Give it here.'

The line went dead.

The needle jumped over the speed limit again.

Thank God I know where to go. Damn this traffic. Nothing from the phone. Phoning back could make things worse.

I shot through the visitors carpark as fast as I dared. Past the 'Residents Only' sign. Jolting over speed humps.

I skidded to a halt alongside the caravan and jumped out. I could hear shouting and thudding inside. No one else was around.

I grabbed the door, expecting it to be locked. It crashed back violently against the side of the van.

'What the—'

A guy with black hair twisted round angrily. Behind him, Jamie lay sobbing, pressed into a corner. She clutched the edges of her shirt and scrunched them together.

I ducked to get inside. The man squared up belligerently.

'Get out!' I gestured towards the door.

Jamie slid away. He grasped at her hair. She screamed, pulled free and fell to the floor. I stepped between them.

Jamie huddled against the wall.

'What's it to you? She your tart?' he sneered.

'I suggest you get out now.' It sounded more confident than I felt.

He was breathing heavily, reeking of beer.

He jerked forward, faking a punch. 'Had you worried, eh?'

I stood my ground, trying to look unconcerned, anxious not to provoke increased aggression. Thankfully I was taller than him. I moved a fraction closer, obliging him to look at me, then motioned towards the door again, with a tilt of the head.

'Back off, mate,' he scowled. He lumbered to the step, deliberately brushing past me.

The tension was instant, as I anticipated him lashing out.

A shrill voice met him as he stepped off onto the grass. 'Can't trust you for a minute, can I?' A woman with two children was out there. 'The kids said you were over here, you useless—' A torrent of abuse followed.

Some spectators appeared outside the caravan, angling themselves to see what was happening.

Silence. I sat down at the table.

Jamie burst into tears.

Fancy crying in front of the deputy. Jamie dabbed at her eyes. Her breathing was still jerky – in snatches. He hadn't really known what to do – in the end he went to get more tissues from his car. Now he was back, hovering at the door.

'Would you like me to ring Ms Davis? She wouldn't mind.'

'I'm all right.' Jamie breathed deeply. 'I'll ring Dominic.'

The phone was on the opposite end of the table, nearest the door. The deputy reached in and slid it towards her.

'It's been doing a bit of overtime, that phone. You get full marks for quick thinking.'

'Couldn't look to check the number,' she admitted, with fewer stuttering breaths. 'I didn't know it was you.'

'So it wasn't a decision to call for a James Bond-type person, with lightning reactions and rally driving skills?'

Faint smile.

'Where were you when I rang?'

'Just leaving school.'

She looked up. 'Did you think you'd make it in time?'

'No. I was a bit worried. That's why I've probably got fines for speeding and reckless driving.'

The deputy produced his own phone. 'I'll give my wife a call, while you ring Dominic.' He stepped aside, out on the grass and started speaking almost immediately. 'Yes, I know I did, but something came up. I . . .' the words were lost as he moved further away.

Jamie sighed, listening to the ring tone. Then everything came out in a rush when Dominic answered. She was still talking as he left Ricky's house and started to run.

'It's a waste of time telling the police.' Jamie protested. 'Nothing'll happen.'

She didn't want to let Rob off, but something was bothering her. 'If it goes any further, we'll have social workers round here causing problems for Dominic and me!'

She could hear her own frustration. Why couldn't the deputy accept what she said?

'I'm not trying to cause problems,' he said quietly. 'I don't have a choice. You're still enrolled at school.'

Jamie remained silent.

'And, at a personal level,' he continued, 'after this, if anything happened to you, or anyone else, it would be on my conscience. I'd have trouble getting to sleep'.

It was Jamie's turn to feel awkward.

The deputy looked at his watch, preparing to leave.

Jamie felt weird as she and Dominic stood facing him. It was an ordinary farewell, but it made them more of a couple. It made the caravan more of a home.

'Keep it simple when you ring me next time,' said the deputy, looking at Jamie. 'Just tell me you're ready to come back to school. See you, Dominic.' He climbed out of the caravan and walked away. Seconds later he reached back in and tucked something between the plastic seat cushion and the bench.

'A small contribution towards a hamburger or something,' he said. 'I think it would do you both good to get out.'

I covered for Jessica Rowan this morning, for the first twenty minutes of Lesson One. Her car broke down on the way to school and she had to wait for roadside assistance.

Aaron Lee was in the class. He wanted to show me something, but I asked him to wait until the class had started working.

I quickly whiteboarded the page references and instructions I'd been given, then checked that everyone was under way.

'So what is it you want to show me, Aaron?'

He handed me a small electronic games unit.

'Stewart bought it for me, for doing so well at the

swimming. Look.' He reached out and pressed one of the buttons.

The game options were replaced by a picture of me, writing on the whiteboard.

'This is the camera.' He pointed to a small lens above the screen.

'So this is what you get up to behind my back.'

'It can store several pictures.'

'Me again?'

'No. I took one of Mum and Stewart, last night, while they weren't looking. They told me to go over it.' He grinned as he held it out for me to see.

'TV a bit boring, was it?' I laughed.

Stewart and his mother had their arms around one another, kissing in the corner of a settee.

Jamie turned up today. She seems older. Perhaps it's just that I know what's happened to her.

I can always find something to say, but at times I feel out of my depth.

I told her that Sharleen at the canteen had heard about the incident with Rob, and that she'd said Jamie could stay with her for a while if she needed somewhere to go.

Jamie was really touched by that. She asked me to thank Sharleen, and said she'd do it herself as well, later on.

I didn't have time to talk for long, so I passed her on to Angela.

Jamie told Angela that she wanted to be sure that things had really settled down before she started school again. When the time came, she'd quit her day job and carry on with evening shifts at some fast-food place. She said that things were 'cool' with Dominic. She wasn't living with him. They were just sharing a caravan to save money. She said she'd go on the Pill if anything changed.

Jamie also said that she thought she and Dominic would be good for each other. They both wanted to make something of their lives.

I couldn't help thinking of potential problems, but I was keen to share her optimism.

Angela asked her if she'd heard anything from the police. She said she had. She'd changed her mind and was pressing charges, and they'd need a statement from me.

Angela gave me an envelope which Jamie had asked her to pass on. It was the money I'd left in the caravan. There was a short note with it, saying that they both appreciated the thought, but they were trying to manage on their own.

Apparently, when Jamie left she took a subject selection booklet for Dominic. She said he was coming back to school next term, enrolling in Year 11.

The turnover rate is incredible in this school. The teachers' roll books are full of crossings out and additional names. Sometimes the reasons are tragic. But this could be good news.

Greg Proden caught up with me to say that he'd seen 'the Joel girl' in the yard, talking to other kids, without a visitor's badge. I asked if he'd spoken to her at all. He said he didn't need to. He could see she didn't have a badge and that was all he needed to know.

I said she'd been in for a meeting and was on her way out again. He said she should have left by the front entrance and walked around the fenceline.

Technically he was correct.

I felt like asking him if he'd ever thought of applying to join the human race.

Jamie knew she hadn't been honest with Ms Davis. She and Dominic weren't full-on living together. But they were more than sharing a caravan.

He hadn't really pressured her for anything more than she was ready to allow. He hadn't got angry so far, when she pulled away and adjusted her clothes. But he went very quiet sometimes.

He'd blow up eventually. Get real moody.

And then what? Was it impossible to keep things as they were?

If they were on the telly, she'd have been astride his naked body by now. Two teenagers just being together, trying to make it work, wouldn't rate. But that's what she wanted most.

Warren Horrowitz came back today after yet another suspension. His mother complained that we ought to keep him at school because he was nothing but trouble when he was home.

We discussed the incident that led to Warren being suspended. Someone in the anger management group said something he didn't like, so he hit him.

'That's not real violence is it?' said Mrs Horrowitz. 'He just hit someone 'cause he had to stick up for himself.'

I've got the feeling I'll be reading about Warren in the newspapers one day, and he's just as likely to be the victim as the aggressor. He's going to make an awful lot of enemies the way he's going.

I asked Warren what he knew about some recent graffiti

the groundsman had taken photos of around the school, then confronted him with similar graffiti in his diary.

He immediately denied doing it. He said he'd seen the graffiti before it was rubbed off and he'd copied it to show some other kids.

I suggested that some of the writing in his diary had been done before the graffiti appeared on the walls.

He was quick to remind me that it was the new diary I'd given him after his first one ended up in the washing machine. He looked quite pleased. Any previous evidence had been washed away. His alibi was strengthening.

He said he hadn't used his new diary to start with. He kept forgetting. He said he'd shown it to his mum not long ago and there was nothing in it.

'That's right, isn't it, Mum? You can ask her.'

'Yeah, that's right. I saw it and there was nothing in it,' said Mrs Horrowitz. 'So it wasn't him what did it. He just copies things. He does it all the time.'

'Will I be able to get all the subjects I want for the second half of the year?' asked Dominic. He was sprawled over the bed, surrounded by information sheets, brochures and blank pro-formas. A Senior School course booklet was open at his side.

'The counsellor thought you would. Not all the classes are full. There are always people dropping out,' said Jamie. 'Like me,' she added, continuing to clear up. 'Only most of them don't go back.'

Jamie peered outside, into the darkness.

Since the incident with Rob, she hadn't been able to face the dark on her own.

'Domini i i i c,' she pleaded.

'Cross your legs and hang on,' he said. 'Promise I won't be more than two hours.'

As Dominic rolled to the side of the bed and swung his legs onto the floor, Jamie's phone rang.

Ricky.

'You're joking! I can't believe it. Are you sure?' Jamie turned to Dominic. Her voice was thin and fragile. 'It's Ricky. Put the radio on.'

I was close to tears this morning. Alex Marlow is dead. It was mentioned on the news. All the kids were talking about it.

He was joy-riding a motorbike he'd stolen. He headed into a makeshift parking area alongside the station, when it was getting dark. They'd recently put a chain across the entrance to block it off, and he didn't see it.

The more I thought about it the worse it got. There are parts of this job that you take inside yourself. You just can't help it.

It was the thought of neither parent wanting him that did it. Would they be at the funeral? What would they be thinking? What would they say to each other?

It was all too depressing to contemplate.

I keep thinking of Jamie's question. 'Did you think you'd make it in time?'

At what stage in events do you make it 'in time'?

As far as some of these kids are concerned no one makes it in time. Certainly not me.

A heap of kids will be at the funeral.

I'll be the official representative from the school.

I'm not sure how I'll cope.

Jamie could see Cheryl, seated at the front of the church, clutching Heath.

The coffin in front of her looked so small. There were three flower arrangements on top.

Jamie recognised the posy she'd chosen. She'd settled for a card with a verse about remembering people. She wouldn't forget Alex helping her get away from Rob. Inside she'd written, *Thanks for your help when I needed it, Alex. I didn't get to say it, but I really mean it. Love, Jamie.*

Alex's bike was propped against the side of the coffin, with a large wreath on the handlebars.

The solemnity of the occasion was engraved on the kids' faces. No one spoke. They did as they were asked, better than they ever would for a school assembly.

Jamie liked what the clergyman said. He wouldn't have known anything about Alex until the last few days, but he didn't make him out to be some innocent little chocolate-box kid. He said Alex had lived a 'troubled' life at times, and had difficulty finding his way. He'd looked after his brother Heath sometimes and helped his mother sort out some problems recently.

In the prayers, the clergyman asked everybody to think of Alex's parents.

Jamie couldn't suppress her thoughts. There were more than a few times when Cheryl had wanted to get rid of Alex, times when she'd wished him dead. How was she dealing with that now?

Perhaps your mind helps you extinguish things you don't want to know.

As Jamie made her way out of the pew she saw Mr Eliot and his wife. He nodded silently as she and Dominic filed past.

Jamie was surprised by a faint smile of recognition from Mrs Eliot. Behind them there were two women in black skirts and white blouses. They probably worked with Cheryl at the pub.

As soon as she was outside, Jamie searched for Cheryl.

'You okay?'

'Only just.'

'What happens next?'

'When the priest's ready he's taking us to the crematorium.'

'Where's Rob?'

'It's all over,' said Cheryl. 'He was shacked up with some other woman. Alex found out. He followed him home one day . . . You know Alex. Rob's got two other kids. Can you believe that?' hissed Cheryl, struggling to keep her voice down. 'Bastard!'

Jamie and Dominic did their best to look surprised.

The greetings I exchanged with kids who had been to the funeral were different today. There was a point of connection – we weren't just stuck in our usual roles. It's the kind of thing I can build on. It might even help when talking to the Horrowitz boys.

Then again, perhaps not.

Cathy Lee spoke to me.

'I don't know her that well,' she said, referring to Mrs Marlow. 'But I do feel for her.'

'Did you know Alex?'

'He turned up at the breakfast program some mornings. Always suspicious. Ready to shoot off. He thought it might be a trap. It was like feeding a stray cat.'

It doesn't take long for things to get back to normal.

Mel Richter was reported for trying to pierce her nose during Maths. She was using a bent paper clip and a compact mirror.

Nick Kelland must be suicidal. He smuggled a hacksaw out of Tech. Studies then was caught trying to saw through a gas pipe in the Science lab.

Ashlee Sinclair admitted herself to the sickroom first thing this morning. She was found fast asleep when a student with a grazed arm needed treatment several hours later. She said she knew there was a bed in there and she was very tired.

Someone threw a hamburger at Gary Hawthorne when he was on yard duty at lunchtime. He had no idea who did it but he wanted the death penalty for Jarrad Hardie. Jarrad rushed up to him straight afterwards and asked, 'Would you like fries with that?'

A group of Year 8 boys admitted peeing out the window of the boys' toilets. Apparently they'd done it before. This was the Grand Final.

What is it about Jason Gillet and Shaun Neale that makes them such idiots? Today they were brought back to school by police officers for the second time this term.

'These two students were found hanging around on the waste land, by the railway track,' explained one of the officers.

'Just after the level crossing?' I asked.

'Yes.' The officer glanced at the boys. They avoided his gaze. 'At a time when they should have been in school, a member of the public reported that these boys were putting things on the track.'

I looked at Jason. He lowered his head with an expression that had 'Guilty' written all over it.

I remembered doing the same thing when I was a boy. We used to put coins on the rails and take great delight in finding them flattened like tinfoil, after the train had gone over them.

'What sort of things?' I inquired.

'The member of the public who reported them is prepared to make a statement,' continued the officer 'They've admitted everything. To start with, they were putting stones and coins on the line. But when we arrived they were busy trying to put something else on the track.' He paused and looked at the boys, 'I don't know what gets into kids like you. You could have derailed the whole train.'

The officer looked at me. 'It could have been a lot worse if we hadn't arrived.'

He turned back to the boys. 'Have you any idea what might have happened if you'd managed to roll that washing machine onto the track?'

Jamie looked at the timetable she'd been sent for next term. She wasn't changing her mind again. Strangely everything seemed clearer since the funeral.

Ms Davis had mailed it with a note asking her to ring Mr Eliot if there were any problems.

She still had Proden for Social Studies. She was tempted to ring about that. She could tell that Mr Eliot didn't think much of him, even though he never said anything personal.

He always talked about getting on with everybody, the world being full of different types of people, and not being able to choose your boss when you went to work.

In some ways it was true. Plenty of other kids managed to put up with Proden.

Every day she remained at school would be a victory for her. It would only take a week for the score to be five-nil. That was one way to look at it.

Dominic would be there. That would really make a difference. He wouldn't just be at the end of the phone. She wouldn't be on her own, struggling to keep Jamie cam' pictures in her mind.

She looked at the wizard.

There were no guarantees in the crystal ball, but when it sparkled in the sunlight – sheer silver and white – she just dared to think that things might work out.

Acknowledgements

I would like to thank the following people who, in so many different ways, provided the help and support that was needed to complete this book: Sarah Brenan, Rosalind Price, Kay Brindal, Linda Dumbleton, Andrew Gordon, Jacinta di Mase, Jenny Darling, Ray Moss, Cate Taylor, Roger Both, Max Fatchen, Fij Miller, Christine Thompson and all the students who read and responded to successive drafts of the manuscript.